I0721812

# DEBORAH GRACE WHITE

**Island of Secrets and Sacrifice**
Sacrificed Hearts Book Four

Copyright © 2023 by Deborah Grace White

First edition (v1.0) published in 2024
by Luminant Publications

All rights reserved. Without limiting the rights under copyright reserved
above, no part of this publication may be reproduced, distributed,
transmitted, stored in, or introduced into a database or retrieval system, in
any form, or by any means, without the prior written permission of both
the copyright owner and the above publisher of this book.

The characters and events portrayed in this book are fictitious. Any
similarity to real persons, living or dead, is coincidental and not intended
by the author.

ISBN: 978-1-925898-83-5

Luminant Publications
PO Box 305
Greenacres, South Australia 5086

http://www.deborahgracewhite.com

Cover Design by Moorbooks Design
Map illustration by Rebecca E. Paavo

*For Talitha*
*May you have the tenacity to stand up against injustice, and the courage to not lose your sunshine in the process.*

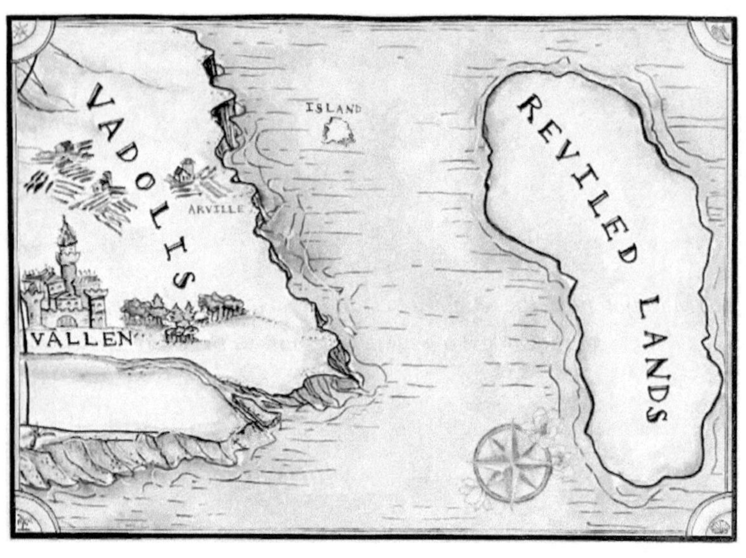

VADOLIS
ARVILLE
VÄLLEN
ISLAND
REVILED LANDS

# PROLOGUE

# Haiden

Haiden crested the hill, grunting in satisfaction as a hamlet came into sight below him. This must be Arville. Beyond the little town, the coastline stretched out from north to south, sunlight sparkling off the expanse of water. His journey to Providore's eastern shore had taken longer than he'd expected, but after months of travel, he'd finally reached his destination.

Or rather, his starting point, if all went to plan. Which it hadn't so far, he reflected ruefully. He remembered thinking, when he slipped away from the Terenan capital where he'd lived for two years, that if his sister knew his plans, she'd tell him seventeen was far too young to venture out on his own.

Some might say his misadventures on the trip through the intervening kingdoms of Frossenland and Vadolis had proved Gisela's caution right. But Haiden was too resilient to take that view. Or perhaps too stubborn. He remained determined to reach his goal without help from his sister or anyone.

It took another hour to reach the hamlet, and by the

time he entered the tiny tavern, he was tired. He hoped they had rooms available. It wasn't a large establishment.

"No children allowed in here, lad," said the barkeep, with a grin.

Haiden glared back. "Very funny."

The man glanced at Haiden's rucksack. "Traveler, are you? Don't get a lot of newcomers around here."

"Yes, I'm a traveler," Haiden said wearily, sinking onto a stool. "And no need to look me over like that. There's nothing of value in my rucksack save a few coins, and I'll give them to you willingly in exchange for a room."

The man chuckled, not offended by the insinuation. "I'm no thief, lad. We're simple folk in Arville, but I reckon we're honest. I can give you a room if you've the coins."

Haiden nodded. "Thank you." He cast his eyes over the room, noting a couple of men seated at a nearby table, chatting over their tankards. "Are they fishermen?"

"Aye." The barkeep resumed wiping out cups. "But then, most everyone around here is a fisherman."

"So I've heard," said Haiden in satisfied tones. "That's why I've come to Arville. I hear the people here know the eastern seas better than anyone. I figure if anyone will take me east, I'll find them here."

"East?" The barkeep paused, frowning in confusion. "You *are* east. This is Providore's eastern shore. There is nothing further east."

"Nothing on Providore," Haiden agreed. He drummed his fingers absently on the counter. "What I'm looking for isn't on this continent."

The barkeep put his cloth down, crossing his arms. "You're talking about the Reviled Lands?"

The conversation at the nearby table petered out, the

two fishermen looking up to listen. Haiden raised his eyebrows.

"It seems I've incited you to utter a forbidden phrase."

"No need to be flippant," the barkeep said disapprovingly. "You're in the wrong place. Just because we fish the eastern sea doesn't mean we're fools who don't know how to leave well enough alone. No one sails toward the Reviled Lands. No one even tries."

"I'm not looking to get anyone in trouble," Haiden said. "I know contact with the Reviled Lands is forbidden. I'm just asking a question."

"Then stop asking," one of the fishermen piped up. "You'll get the same answer from everyone in Arville. The ban on communication with the Reviled Lands is the least of our concerns. You can't sail east more than about fifty nautical miles without running afoul of the magic."

Haiden swiveled in his chair, his attention fully caught. "What magic?"

"The people of Providore aren't the only ones who don't want contact between the two lands," the other fisherman said. "When the Reviled Lands fell, they set up a magical barrier, to prevent anyone from Providore interfering with them. We leave it be."

Haiden frowned. "I've never heard anything of that."

The fisherman scoffed. "And why would you? You're clearly from one of the western kingdoms. What do you know of the Reviled Lands?"

Haiden kept his peace. His audience would be unimpressed if he told them that he was motivated primarily by curiosity. And there was no need to tell them that he had his own particular reasons for that curiosity—he didn't wish to reveal details of his ancestry to these strangers.

Somebody else deemed it time to become involved in

the conversation, however. The high-pitched chuckle brought Haiden's head whipping around. He hadn't realized there was an elf in the tavern, sitting well back in the shadows on the far side of the room.

The elf stood, his height as a fully grown adult about half Haiden's. Like all of his kind, he had alabaster skin and emerald green eyes. He strolled forward in a leisurely way, looking Haiden over. Haiden eyed the streaks of gray in the elf's hair. He was middle aged, it seemed, which for an elf, meant much older than the human equivalent.

"Oho, you've an air about you, that's certain." The elf grinned at Haiden. "Asking very interesting questions, too. I'd love to know your interest in the Reviled Lands."

"Would you?" Haiden responded, the words covered by the thinnest veneer of politeness.

The elf chuckled again. "Too wise to give information away for free, are you? I'd hazard a guess you've dealt with elves before."

Haiden's face communicated nothing, but internally he grimaced. The elf's guess was a drastic understatement. Haiden's whole life had been shaped by dealings with elves. One in particular, little as she'd intended to shatter his world.

"Yes, I see you have." The elf sounded fascinated now. "I suspected as soon as you walked in that you were a singer, but that doesn't account for the trace of power that lingers around you. It's not your own, is it? It's...something else."

"Here we go." The barkeep's mutter suggested the locals didn't have much patience for elves and their mystical, cryptic ways, and Haiden felt a surge of fellow feeling with the man.

It wasn't that Haiden minded the elf identifying him as a singer—he had no reason to hide the fact that he'd been born with that rare magical ability. But he didn't like the elf probing into this supposed *trace of power*. Whatever it was, it wasn't Haiden's singing gift. Singers might be able to channel magic from the ground, but they didn't walk around leaking power that others could detect.

"I know what it is." The pointed tips of the elf's ears quivered with excitement as he deciphered what he was feeling. "It's an elf prophecy. You've been the recipient of one, haven't you?"

An icy chill rushed over Haiden, and this time he had to work hard to keep his face neutral. The words struck at the heart of his greatest fear, and for a moment he felt like a helpless, confused child again.

*No!* he shouted internally. *I'm in charge of my own life. I will* not *let idle words from an elf control my destiny ever again.*

"I don't know what you mean," he said gruffly, turning back to the bar.

The elf made a noise of satisfaction. "Yes, you do. Where are you from that you've brushed shoulders with elf royalty?"

"Elves don't have royalty," said Haiden shortly, still not looking at the creature.

"I'm using a human word to convey my meaning to the less-than-subtle minds of your species," said the elf impatiently. "You know what I mean. A prophecy powerful enough to leave a mark like that didn't come from just any elf."

"There's no mark," said Haiden, growing angry. "You don't know what you're talking about."

The elf looked him over disapprovingly. "Don't know what I'm talking about? You'd be wise to heed the advice of your betters, human stripling."

"I didn't ask for your advice," said Haiden shortly. "And

I'm not afraid of your kind. I know plenty about the ways of elves, and if you expect reverence, look elsewhere." He glanced scornfully around the tavern. "Living a little far from any elf community, aren't you? Which means you're most likely an outcast or a nutter."

"Easy, lad," said the barkeep placatingly. "No need to make it personal."

"He already did that," said Haiden, unrepentant.

His breath was coming quickly, his anger fueled by shame at his own reaction to the claim that the elf prophecy from his childhood still left a mark. He was too gripped by his emotions to listen to what his better sense was telling him—that while elves were shrewd to a point most humans considered unscrupulous, they weren't usually prone to outbursts of temper. This was an elf of a different kind from the ones he'd dealt with. There was undoubtedly a reason he was an outcast from his own people, and a cautious man would probably have avoided offending him.

But Haiden had clearly passed that point. The elf's anger now matched his own, suggesting he'd struck a nerve with his observation about the stranger's isolation.

"You insolent worm," said the elf. "You know nothing about me. You're clearly adrift at sea in your own life's journey, let alone being an authority on anyone else's."

"I'm not adrift," Haiden contradicted. "I know exactly where I'm going."

The elf gave a derisive laugh. "Yes, to the Reviled Lands, apparently. Go right ahead, whelp. Keep telling yourself you're seeking something. Deep down, you know you're actually running from something. But the mark will follow you wherever you go. If you try to run from it, you'll only become the monster you fear you already are."

Haiden's hot retort was stilled as he felt a rush of power

issue from the elf with the words. A sharp cry from the barkeep followed immediately. Was the man also a singer, to have felt the magic that had issued from the elf and broken over Haiden? But the barkeep's eyes were fixed on something in the elf's hand.

"What's that you're holding?" he demanded. "You know the rules—no elven talismans in here!"

"Talisman?" Haiden demanded sharply, searching the elf's form. The miniature creature was slipping his hands into his pockets, his expression smug. Haiden caught a glimpse of a black stone, threaded through with red and purple that glinted in the candlelight. "What did you do to me?"

"Nothing," the elf said with an exaggerated air of innocence. "You'll do it all to yourself. You need no one's help getting there."

"That's right," Haiden shot back, fear and anger still pulsing through him. "I *do* need no one's help."

Chuckling nastily, the elf strode toward the door, hands still buried in his pockets. Haiden watched him go through narrowed eyes, trying to ignore how uneasy the encounter had made him feel.

"How about that room then, eh?" The barkeep sounded discomfited himself.

"Forget it." Haiden glanced out the window. There were still a few hours until sunset. "I'm not staying here. I'll leave today."

"Leave where?" The barkeep frowned at him. "You can't sail to the Reviled Lands, lad. We weren't joking about the magical protection on the waters to the east. You can't get past it. If you try, the magic will kill you."

"When's the last time someone tested that claim and fell afoul of this supposed protection?" Haiden's challenging stare encompassed the listening fishermen as well.

There was silence in the tavern.

"Are there any singers in your community, to confirm the existence of the magic?"

Still no one spoke, and Haiden made a noise in his throat. "That's what I thought. You can suit yourselves, but I don't intend to be ruled by superstition."

He strode from the tavern, clutching his rucksack to his shoulder with one clenched fist. Those men might be too timid to help him, but surely he'd find someone else willing to do it.

He soon discovered this optimism to be misplaced. No one in Arville would even consider sailing further east than their usual fishing grounds. Still gripped by the reckless anger brought on by the encounter with the elf, Haiden formed a new plan. He'd said from the start of his journey that he didn't need anyone's help. The superstitious folk of Arville were no exception.

Gathering the coins from his rucksack—plus the larger stash hidden in his boots—he made an impulsive purchase. The small wooden boat was old but serviceable, its sail in passable condition, and some worn sections reinforceable by a simple song of mending.

He examined the supplies he'd stashed in the storage compartment. They were enough to last at least a week at sea. He hadn't come this far to turn back without even trying to reach the Reviled Lands.

His ears ringing with the warnings of every inhabitant of Arville whom he'd encountered, Haiden set out an hour before sunset. The sea was smooth, the tide propitious, and the skies clear.

Even so, the long, cold night on the water gave him

plenty of opportunity to question the wisdom of his rash departure. But his spirit wasn't so easily broken. He was still clinging to wakefulness when morning broke.

More confident in finding his direction during the day, he allowed himself to doze for a couple of hours, his boat still moving steadily eastward. When he awoke, the sun indicated that it was mid-morning.

Haiden shook himself, his mind foggy and his limbs sore. He didn't have a very clear idea of how long it would take to sail to the Reviled Lands, even if the conditions remained as incredibly favorable as they currently were.

He peered eastward, noting with surprise that there was the barest smudge on the horizon. Could he be approaching his destination already? But no, the land mass didn't look big enough to be another continent.

There was no warning. One moment, he was sailing through open water, his eyes fixed on the smudge, and the next he'd slammed into a wall of pure power. It crashed over him, sending him thudding to the floor of his little vessel, momentarily paralyzed. The magic ripped through his body, his senses as a singer recognizing it through the excruciating pain that assaulted every inch of him.

Blackness clawed at his vision, his mind screaming for unconsciousness to release him from the pain. But he could feel the magic pouring relentlessly into him, and he feared that if he passed out, he would never wake. He had to get away from the invisible wall of power.

Venting his agony in a scream of pain and effort, he dragged himself back up and grabbed at the ropes. He hauled on them, bringing the boat slowly and tortuously around westward. He felt the moment he cleared the magic barrier, but to his dismay, pain still burned over him in increasingly unbearable waves.

He tied off the rope, hope leaking from him as the boat made only labored progress through the water, and consciousness faded.

The last thing he was aware of, other than the crippling pain, was his own voice, raised feebly in an instinctive response as he attempted a song of healing over his own drooping form.

It wasn't enough to stop the darkness from taking him.

**CHAPTER ONE**

# Ember

"Ember! Come inside, now! Don't make me ask again."

With a sigh, Ember turned away from the gloriously painted sky, scrunching up her face as she obeyed her mother's command.

"Relax, Mother," she said, entering the neat stone home she'd lived in all her life. "I'm coming."

"Why must you always push the boundary with curfew?" her mother complained. "You're turning me gray before my time, Em. The rule has always been the same. Why is it so hard to remember you're not supposed to be outside after dark?"

"It's not dark," Ember protested. "I was watching the sunset. Meaning, the sun hasn't yet set."

Her mother was unimpressed. "You can watch the sunset through the window, Ember."

Ember didn't bother to contradict. What was the point? If her mother needed her to explain why seeing the sunset through filmy glass wasn't the same as breathing in the fresh salt air as the sun sank riotously into the ocean beyond the western cliffs where their home perched, then she'd never understand the explanation.

"Hold on," she said, frowning at the plates her mother was laying out. "Why are you setting a fourth place for dinner?" She looked suspiciously at her mother, who was glancing out the door. "And why are you watching impatiently for Father to come home?"

"Your father is bringing a guest tonight," said her mother with dignity.

Ember narrowed her eyes. "Who?"

"Don't start this again, Ember," her mother said warningly.

"Mother! It's Gil, isn't it?" Ember said in frustration. "Why are you pushing this so hard?"

"Because Gil is an incredibly nice young man, who's prepared to provide you with a stable and productive future," her mother replied. "You know our opinion. I expect the matter to be settled tonight."

"But I don't want to marry Gil!" Ember protested. "Doesn't that count for anything?"

"We've taken your opinion into consideration," her mother told her. "But you're young, Ember. You think you know what you want, but trust me, your priorities will change in time. And with Gil, you'll have a happy and safe home. He's a good man. It's not as though we're trying to push you onto someone cruel."

"If I'm so young, why the hurry to marry me off?" Ember said desperately.

Her mother gave her a look. "You know what I mean. Nineteen is plenty old enough to marry. We've settled all the details with Gil's parents. His father is to gift him extra land on your marriage, isn't it wonderful?"

"No," said Ember emphatically. "It's not wonderful. Mother, I don't want to spend my life as a farmer's wife!"

"Then what?" her mother snapped. "You don't want to marry someone who works the mine like your father, either. Most people on the island are farmers or miners. What's this special destiny you think you should find?"

Ember pressed her lips together mutinously. She knew better than to say what she was thinking. But her mother read her silent answer anyway, and a storm grew on the other woman's brow.

"Ember, don't be a fool," she said sharply. "All that nonsense about wanting to leave the island is a childish fancy you need to forget. No one leaves the island. No one *wants* to leave the island."

"I do," Ember muttered.

"No you don't," her mother contradicted quickly. "You just think you do, because you don't understand what you're really dreaming about. We're safe on the island. There's nothing to the east but the ravaged land our ancestors fled, and nothing to the west but the mainland that hunted our fleeing people like animals. If you go in either direction, you'll find only persecution and death."

Ember put the pitcher of water on the table with unnecessary force.

"How do you know that? How does anyone know that? No one's tried leaving in decades."

"The Protector left," her mother countered. "He risked his life to sail to the mainland when our ancestors' magical protection around our island failed. A boat from the mainland actually reached our shores, with armed men ready to kill any within reach!"

"Yes, Mother, I know the story," said Ember. "The former

Protector and his sons fought the intruders off." She was unimpressed by this mention of the community's chief leader.

"And then the Protector set out to find a new solution to keep us safe," her mother reminded her. "No one else was willing to risk their lives, but he did it, even though he was so young then. And he saw firsthand what a vile and lawless place the mainland is."

"So he claims," Ember muttered.

"Ember!" Her mother's shock at this mutiny was genuine, and Ember sighed.

"Even if it was as bad as he said, that was thirty years ago. Maybe things have improved since then."

"The land was overrun with savage monsters and even more savage humans," her mother said, aghast. "And the moment they learned he was descended from the land of our ancestors, they turned on him. He barely escaped with his life, and it was only thanks to his shrewd negotiation that he found a monster whose services could be bought, and that our island remains protected."

Ember pursed her lips. "Well, maybe he saw a particularly bad corner of the mainland," she argued. "Maybe most people wouldn't care where we're from."

"Don't talk such foolishness," said her mother, growing visibly distressed. "Our leaders know what they're talking about, and they only have our safety in mind. I tell you, there's good reason why no one leaves the safety of the island."

"Not no one," Ember said, unable to help herself. "The tributes sacrificed to the monster leave."

"Don't speak of that." Her mother's hand was unsteady as she put a basket of still-steaming bread in the center of the table. "It's a necessity no one relishes."

Ember raised her eyebrows. "You're the one who brought up the Protector's *shrewd negotiation*. You call it a necessity, but how do we know that's the only way to keep us safe? Do you think Diana's parents would call it a necessity?"

Her mother's face was more troubled now, and she wouldn't look Ember in the eye. "It's been three years since Diana left, Ember. There's nothing to be gained from speaking of it. We can only be thankful the monster didn't demand a sacrifice more regularly than every five years. And that it's still fulfilling its promise to guard the eastern shore of the mainland and prevent anyone from discovering us here."

"We should be grateful, should we?" Again, Ember was unimpressed. "How do we even know that there *is* a monster, or that it's doing its part?"

"What a question."

Her mother still wasn't meeting Ember's gaze. Like the rest of the island, the older woman usually avoided discussing the tradition of sacrifice, seeing it as an unfortunate necessity not to be dwelled on.

"We know," Ember's mother went on, "because no one else from the mainland has ever breached our border since the Protector's mission. If the monster wasn't doing its part, the mainlanders would have found us by now."

"Well, I don't feel grateful," Ember said stubbornly. "Even if you're right about the monster being real, for all we know, we don't even want it to keep our existence secret anymore. What if the mainland could help us? The island is becoming crowded, and we're already struggling to grow enough crops to feed everyone."

"Help us?" her mother repeated, horrified. "We don't want their help. They hunted survivors from our ancestors' homeland for sport. I'm daily grateful *our* ancestors were lucky enough to find this island when they fled, instead of being forced to continue to the mainland. And our resources aren't dwindling. The mine has plenty of regal onyx still to be found."

"We can't eat onyx," said Ember, blowing an unruly curl of red hair out of her eyes. "All I'm saying is I'd like to speak to this monster. I'd have a few thoughts to share on offering to 'protect' us at the cost of the lives of innocent girls."

Her mother let out a cry of protest. "Speak to the monster? Don't say such things, Ember! That kind of dangerous talk is exactly why your father and I are determined to see you married and secure as soon as possible! Gil will protect you from yourself even if we can't talk sense into you."

Ember scowled, but before she could reply, the sound of men's voices drifted through the open doorway.

"They're here," her mother said. Her voice turned pleading. "Don't do anything to make him change his mind, Ember. You've always had a knack for attracting the wrong kind of attention. With Gil, you've finally gained attention worth having, so don't ruin it for yourself."

There was no time for more. The strong footsteps of Ember's father were at the door, a younger man following close behind him. With a sour taste in her mouth, Ember greeted the farmer politely, reminding herself that it wasn't his fault her parents had selected him to tame her rebellious ways. She knew she didn't have the ability to prevent the marriage, so she'd be a fool to antagonize him from the start.

He was even good-looking, she reflected glumly, in a fair-haired, non-threatening sort of way. He was strong and well-built, and she had no doubt he would father hearty, healthy, compliant children, who would work the land and follow the rules.

The prospect did nothing to excite her.

"Well, Ember." Her father beamed at her. "This is a happy occasion." He clapped his prospective son-in-law on the shoulder. "Gil and I come ready to celebrate, don't we?"

"I couldn't agree more," said Gil, his voice deep and calming. He dipped his head to Ember, his gaze a little shy. "I'm so pleased to have reached an agreement, and I look forward with anticipation to our future together."

*An agreement with whom?* Ember didn't say the words aloud, but in her heart, mutiny was in full swing. She couldn't even bring herself to return her father's greeting. He knew perfectly well it wasn't a happy occasion as far as she was concerned. There was a reason her parents had waited until the last moment to tell her Gil was coming, rather than giving her enough warning to find a way out of the evening's plans.

"Let me wash up, and then we'll drink to the future," Ember's father said, apparently finding nothing to disapprove of in Gil's matter-of-fact and unromantic proposal.

He strode from the room to freshen up after a day of working in the mine that occupied the island's northern region. The precious stone mined there was found nowhere but the island, its excavation closely regulated given it served as their currency. It was a beautiful jet black, with glowing threads of red and purple, royal colors which had earned it the nickname of regal onyx.

"Thank you, Antoine, Hetta." Gil smiled at Ember's mother. "I trust it will be the first of many meals together." He sent a tentative smile in Ember's direction as well, but try as she might, she couldn't return it.

Her parents would no doubt think she was being melodramatic, but she really thought the prospect of eating every meal with this solid, unimaginative farmer for the rest of her life might just break her heart.

# CHAPTER TWO

# Ember

Ember rose early the next morning, her mood somber. Her parents were both delighted with the success of the evening's dinner, and full of plans for a simple wedding in a matter of weeks. Ember took no part in these discussions, feeling that if she opened her mouth to speak, the rising panic might escape in a scream.

"Oh, I have to go to market this morning." The abrupt comment from Ember's mother provided a very welcome change in topic.

"But it's not our market day," Ember said, surprised. Life on the island followed the same routine every week without deviation. "You went yesterday."

"Yes, I did," her mother agreed. "But I miscalculated and was short how many eggs I needed for the fishmonger. He kindly gave me the fish anyway, and I said I'd bring the extra eggs today."

"I can take them," Ember offered quickly, eager for the opportunity to escape their property. "I know where the fishmonger's stall is."

"Thank you, Ember, that would be a great help."

Her mother handed over a basket, and Ember wasted no time in visiting the spacious chicken coop situated behind their house.

Ten minutes later, she was on her way to the market, although not by the most direct route. Instead she wound her way along the top of the steep cliffs, listening to the ocean pounding against the stone far below.

What she loved most about the cottage she shared with her parents was its proximity to the island's western cliffs. Her mother said that it had driven her to distraction when Ember was a small child, trying to prevent her from tumbling over the edge. But Ember considered the danger worth it for the many hours of her childhood she'd spent exploring the cliffs and gazing westward.

Perhaps if she lived on the island's eastern edge, her curiosity would have been awakened more in regard to the wasteland from which her ancestors had fled. But Ember didn't wonder much about the land the singers had destroyed with their greed and violence. Whenever she dreamed about adventure, it was on the mainland, discovering a new land and a new way of life. The existence of monsters might put her mother off, but it told Ember that magic existed elsewhere than their island.

Not that life on the island involved a great deal of magic. Ember had once awaited with great eagerness the little displays of power that enlivened seasonal festivals and the like. But now they seemed meaningless. If the island really did confer magic on its chosen leaders, why did they use it to make pretty fireworks displays, instead of addressing the various shortages that were making life more complicated by the year?

The main village came into view, and Ember peeled away from the cliffs. The market was in full swing, sounds of the bustle reaching her ears before she caught sight of the stalls. The market operated on two days of the week, with half the island's population assigned to each day. She looked around her with interest at those neighbors who didn't share her usual day. With a smile, she spotted Noani, a girl her own age with whom she'd been friendly in school days. They rarely saw each other now, with Noani's home duties occupying most of her time.

"Noani!" Ember hurried toward her friend, waving her basket in greeting.

"Ember." The other girl smiled, hoisting her baby higher on her hip. "I haven't seen you in an age. What brings you to market today?"

"An excellent question."

The new voice forestalled Ember's answer, and both girls turned to see a grizzled man approaching. He wore a broad smile clearly designed to put them at ease, but like always, it made Ember's skin crawl.

"Leave us be," she muttered as he approached, too low for him to hear.

"Ember!"

Noani didn't need to say more. Her hiss carried with it the words she'd scolded Ember with every time this man had visited their school to encourage their efforts and hear their recitals. Like their peers, Noani thought Ember should show more respect to a man who was second only to the Protector. He was not only chief assistant, but brother to the Protector, born into the ruling family.

Convenient how they were both chosen by the magic, Ember thought mutinously.

"It's so pleasant to see you, Ember," the Protector's brother continued. "I trust your parents are well."

"They are, thank you," said Ember politely.

"I interrupted your conversation," the man said, his voice still gratingly genial. "I believe Noani asked what brought you here today. Yesterday was, I believe, your family's assigned market day?"

"Yes, sir," said Ember tightly. "My mother came yesterday. But she was short on the eggs required to buy fish, and procured them with a promise to bring the extra eggs today."

"Ahhh, I think I know why she was eager to have them at once," the Protector's brother said. He shot Ember a wink that sent a tiny shudder down her spine. "You had an important dinner last night, I believe."

Ember gritted her teeth behind her polite smile. How did he know about that? And why did he care?

"Allow me to be the first to offer my congratulations," he said. "And to assure you that the Protector wholeheartedly approves of the match."

"I assumed as much," said Ember. "Or I can't imagine my parents would have arranged it."

He didn't seem to catch the note of resentment. "Well said."

"Match?" Noani repeated, her eyes lighting up with excitement. "You never said a word, Ember!"

"Very discreet." The Protector's brother chuckled.

Ember said nothing, irked by his enthusiasm. If he retained any memory of the frustrations she'd caused her teacher in her school days, he was probably as eager to see her married and settled as her parents were. She'd always had a habit of asking uncomfortable questions.

"Well, don't let me keep you from your business," the man said, sending them another benign smile. "Please tell your mother that in these special circumstances, we are more than prepared to overlook the irregularity with the market days."

Ember bit her lip, wondering if she was too suspicious to read a warning into the message.

"What an honor to be so singled out for congratulations by the Protector's right-hand man," Noani gushed, when they were alone again.

Well, alone but for the baby Noani was bouncing on her hip. He was very cute, Ember acknowledged begrudgingly to herself. But not so cute she wanted one of Gil's on her hip.

"I suppose so," she said unenthusiastically.

"Come on, Ember." Noani's kind face grew frustrated. "Don't make me pull it out of you. Your parents have arranged a match! Who is it?"

Ember sighed. "It's Gil."

"Gil?" Noani looked even more excited. "That's wonderful! We'll be neighbors!" She paused, frowning slightly. "Why do you look so glum?"

"Because I don't want to marry Gil," said Ember frankly. She saw that her friend looked horrified, and hastened to add, "It's nothing against him. I'm sure he's very nice. But I don't want to marry a farmer and spend my days tending to his little plot of land."

Noani's distressed expression had changed to a long-suffering one. "That's exactly what I'm doing, Ember, and believe it or not, I'm very happy."

Ember summoned a smile for her friend. "I don't doubt it, Noani. I don't mean to disparage your life. But I've never seen myself as a farmer's wife. And," she added pointedly, "you and your husband did have the benefit of having already fallen in love."

"It was very convenient," Noani acknowledged with a

grin. Her voice turned more serious. "But my parents weren't a love match, you know, and they're happy. The love came later."

"As it did for my parents," said Ember, staring unseeingly into the crowd. "But..." She trailed off, unable to find the words to express the depth of dissatisfaction she felt at the life stretching before her. "I sometimes wonder what would happen if I just *refused* to marry him."

She said the words half to herself, but Noani drew in a sharp breath.

"Ember, you can't do that! A match formalized by your parents! Approved by the Protector himself!"

"I know I can't," sighed Ember. "It would crush my parents, and I don't want to do that." She added recklessly, "But I don't know what the Protector's approval has to do with anything. I can't see any reason why my marriage is any of his business."

A cleared throat made both girls turn, and Noani bobbed respectfully at the sight of a gray-haired woman whose job it was to oversee the market. Reluctantly, Ember did likewise.

"A word, Ember," the woman said in a motherly tone that did nothing to lessen Ember's irritation at the blatant eavesdropping. "I couldn't help overhearing what you just said."

*But you could help inserting yourself into the conversation.* Ember didn't say it aloud.

"Firstly, allow me to offer my congratulations. Gil is a very worthy man, and I'm sure you'll take good care of each other."

"Thank you," said Ember stiffly.

"And please allow me to drop you a word of caution," the

older woman continued. "You're young, but no longer so young that careless talk can be excused on the basis of inexperience. The Protector is a wise and good leader, who has dedicated his life to serving and protecting the people of our island. It does you no credit to disregard his wisdom in such an important life decision." Her gaze was piercing as it pinned Ember. "And speaking disrespectfully of our leaders in the public marketplace does more than just damage your own reputation. It has the potential to lessen—most unjustly—the well-founded faith our people have in our leadership. And, in turn, to lessen the strength and unity of our whole community."

"She's right, Ember," Noani murmured.

With the skills born of long practice, Ember held her tongue. The rebuke was familiar.

"In fact," the woman continued relentlessly, "that kind of disrespect was where the singers' rebellion began. And we all know the misery and violence that led to."

Noani clucked sympathetically, but Ember just felt impatient.

"I'm not a singer," she said. "I have my faults, like anyone. But I've never felt the urge to kill another human being. I wasn't born with the capacity to take a life."

"Of course not," said the older woman indulgently. "Only singers are born with that darkness in their hearts, and we can all be thankful no one with singing blood was among our ancestors who reached this island. But my point is that encouraging disrespect of our great leaders can cause more harm than you intend or understand."

"I didn't mean to encourage disrespect," Ember said mildly.

"I'm sure you didn't, child." The gray-haired woman smiled, as if they'd reached an accord.

Ember recognized the pointlessness of further speech. "Thank you for your wisdom," she said woodenly.

"Of course, my dear." The older woman inclined her head. "Your elders are here to help and guide you. I hope you know that."

"I really must discharge my mother's errand with the fishmonger," Ember said. "She'll be expecting me home."

"Of course," Noani said. "Congratulations again, Ember."

"Thank you," Ember said dully. "It was good to see you, Noani."

She moved away, all her interest in the market gone. She quickly handed the eggs over to the fishmonger and made her way out of the crowded space, trying to pretend she didn't notice the same woman deep in conversation with the Protector's brother.

*You've always had a knack for attracting the wrong kind of attention.*

Her mother's words from the night before danced across her memory. Maybe she was right. Maybe they all were. But if the life they had here was really so good, why couldn't Ember enjoy it? Why did she feel stifled at every turn?

Once she'd left the market square, Ember slowed her pace. She took a different route out of town, trying to enjoy the sunshine while contemplating the future laid out before her. She was well past the main cluster of buildings when the sweet sound of birdcalls slowed her steps even further. She loved to listen to the birds. Their calls were soothing in a way no human voice ever could be.

She paused under a large oak tree, laden with glorious white flowers. A pair of blackbirds were nesting in its branches, one of them swooping back and forth on some errand. Ember listened rapt as they called to each other, their cries lifting her spirits. At least when married to Gil, she'd still be able to hear the birds call.

An idea flashed through Ember's mind, from what origin she couldn't tell. Not so much an idea as an impulse. One which, having been felt, simply refused to be denied. Feeling half foolish, half exhilarated, Ember raised her own voice and attempted to mimic the blackbirds' call. She'd never heard anyone do that before, never tried it herself. At first her voice sounded grating, comically so. But the impulse was still there, so she tried again.

The birds ignored her. But to Ember's ears, her call sounded better the second time. After a few more attempts, she was quite pleased with her efforts.

A thrill passed over her. Who knew a human could make a call like a bird's? And who knew it would feel so good? It was as though a weight was lifted from her shoulders with the sound, like something in her was being set as free as the birds that soared so gladly through the skies. It was quite possibly the most delightful thing she'd ever done.

"What are you doing?"

The harsh voice made Ember jump. She'd been sure she was alone, except for the birds. She spun around to see the Protector's brother emerging from the nearby scrub. For a moment she just stared at him, confused. Had he followed her from the market? Surely not. He was far too important a person to take so much interest in her movements.

"I said, what are you doing?"

Ember felt the hairs on the back of her neck stand up. His broad smile and soothing tones were gone.

"I...I was trying to copy the blackbirds' call," she said stupidly.

"Why?" he demanded, his eyes narrowed.

"For...for fun?"

The answer came out as a question, Ember's heart thumping against her chest. Some instinct was telling her to run, but she pushed it down. She was being dramatic, as usual. Being frowned upon by the island's leaders was nothing new for her. Why did she feel a thrill of fear she'd never felt before?

The grizzled man looked her over, his expression calming slightly as he took in her demeanor. His voice, however, remained stern, and he still held himself tensely.

"You shouldn't do that. It's not a seemly way for a human to behave."

Ember just stared at him, completely at a loss for how to respond to the rebuke.

"You go on home," the man prompted. "Speak of this to no one. No need for others to know of your misdemeanor."

Not trusting herself to speak, Ember hoisted her empty basket up her arm and hurried away. Her heart was still going at double time when she reached home, but she didn't need the leader's warning to keep the encounter to herself. She didn't like to think what her mother would make of it. She'd probably just worry that it would put Gil off the marriage.

Ember still felt unsettled when she went to bed that night, and she slept fitfully. The morning brought no relief. Ember was shaken awake in the early dawn, her mother's ashen face telling her at once that something was wrong.

"What is it?" she asked, sitting upright. "Is one of the farms on fire again?"

Her mother shook her head. "We've been summoned to the market square."

A thrill of fear shot through Ember. Was she to be punished for yesterday's incident? The Protector's brother had seemed very angry, but surely he wouldn't punish her parents as well. "Not just me?" she asked. "You and Father as well?"

Her mother's brow creased in confusion. "Not only our family," she clarified. "Everyone. The Protector has called a gathering of the whole community."

Ember looked out her window, where dawn was only just reaching across the sky. "Now?"

Her mother nodded, looking close to tears. "They couldn't delay. I'm afraid the news is the worst, Ember." She paused, swallowing audibly. "The monster has demanded another sacrifice."

# CHAPTER THREE

# Ember

Ember stared at her mother, barely comprehending. Another sacrifice? That couldn't be right. It was supposed to be every five years. They still had two years until the next one.

"Get dressed, Ember," her mother urged her. "It won't win any favor if we're late."

Ember frowned at her mother's words, although she hastened to obey. Win favor? The sacrifices were chosen by the magic. It shouldn't make any difference whether they were out of favor with the leaders. Even so, she had to admit she was rattled by the monster's demand coming so soon after the previous day's encounter. Surely the beast couldn't see them from the mainland...surely it couldn't somehow know of whatever crime had so offended the Protector's brother the day before.

Her father awaited them outside the house. He said nothing as he looked his wife and daughter over with a tight nod, but Ember could read the anxiety in his frame. Her parents exchanged tense looks as they began to walk, and

Ember realized they were wishing they'd been quicker in arranging her match with Gil.

Traditionally, the magic chose young, unmarried women as sacrifices. If Ember had already been married to Gil, she'd be in no danger of being chosen.

Was it a sign of madness that even now she didn't regret still being free? A bizarre feeling flashed through her, almost anticipation. She remembered telling her mother, only days before, that the only ones who left the island were the doomed sacrifices. Was she...*hoping* to be chosen?

Of course not. That was utterly ridiculous, even for her.

The family reached the market square as the sun rose over the silent crowd. There were no stalls today, no bustle.

Everyone's faces were tense and fearful, none more so than the families of the island's unmarried girls. There were enough of them that Ember's odds should have been good. And yet, a sense of imminent doom was so thick around her that she could barely draw in breath.

"My dear friends."

The Protector's somber voice caused everyone to go still. All eyes flew to the small dais permanently in place at one end of the market square. The community's leader stood regally atop the platform, his hands raised in a gesture of appeal.

"You know it is my great honor to serve you all. But it is with sorrow that I undertake this morning the most difficult of all my duties."

Ember swallowed, telling herself it was mere fancy that made it seem like the Protector's eyes avoided her as they swept the crowd. Even in the distressing circumstances, most people gazed back at him with a faith that savored of adoration. He'd always been their rock and anchor, and never exposed them to any risks that weren't absolutely necessary. They believed he would guide them through this crisis as safely as anyone could.

For her part, guilty as she felt for it, Ember could conjure no warmth for the man who had, like his father before him, been chosen by the magic to lead the island community. He was a familiar figure, but an aloof one. He'd never spoken to her personally, as his brother had on numerous occasions. The Protector always officiated community ceremonies, and made big announcements. But the rest of the time, he stayed out of sight and let his underlings carry out the practical aspects of leadership.

"But even as we grieve the necessity of this moment," the Protector went on, his voice the perfect blend of confidence and gentleness, "we can take solace in this: whoever forfeits their life will not do so in vain. Their sacrifice will protect our community for years to come, and allow us all to prosper in safety. It is, perhaps, the greatest service a person can do for our people. The chosen one will carry with them the deepest gratitude of each one of us."

Ember glanced around to see what the crowd made of this comfort. She saw a few somber nods, but it didn't seem to have softened the tension on the faces of those actually in danger of losing a loved one to the monster. Ember also noticed that the Protector's brother was nowhere to be seen. Another flash of unease went through her.

"We will not draw out this unpleasant process," the Protector said.

He stepped off the dais, the crowd shifting to create a clear space where he could reach the ground. The Protector knelt on one knee, closing his eyes and pressing both palms against the ground.

"Magic," he said gravely, the words an invocation. "We

trust you to guide us. We will honor your selection and endeavor to be worthy of that person's sacrifice."

Ember had thought the crowd silent before, but the hush that fell now was almost stifling. She was so focused on the Protector, it took several long seconds to realize how many people were now looking at her.

Gasps and mutters passed through the crowd, and Ember heard, as if through a long tunnel, her mother begin to cry. The Protector looked up at last, his eyes instantly finding her and holding her in a piercing gaze. Tearing her eyes away, she looked down. Her whole body was glowing, as if lit from within.

"The magic," the Protector's voice was heavy with authority, "has chosen." He inclined his head to Ember. "We honor your sacrifice."

"We honor your sacrifice." The murmur passed through the crowd, none of whom would meet Ember's eye.

She caught sight of Noani, standing beside her husband and clutching her baby in her arms as tears leaked down her face. Ember's gaze skated over the crowd, catching on Gil next.

Poor Gil. The devastation on his face was touching. And he, at least, was looking right at her. His evident heartbreak convinced Ember that he really had wanted to marry her. It should bring grief, probably, but she couldn't seem to feel anything. She was curiously numb, everything muffled and distant, neither fear nor defiance yet discernible in her mind. She certainly didn't consider trying to fight the selection. It had been clear and undeniable. And somehow, bizarrely, she felt as if she'd always known it would come to this.

Then her eyes found her parents, and at last some

emotion broke through. It was impossible to be unmoved at the sight of their faces.

"Ember." Her mother's whisper cut right into Ember's heart, propelling her back into motion.

"It's all right, Mother," she said earnestly. "I swear, it'll be all right." She embraced the older woman fiercely. "I said I wanted to speak with the monster, didn't I?"

Her mother was weeping openly. "You should never have said that," she sobbed.

Ember placed her hands on either side of her mother's face, her serious gaze encompassing her father as well. "Listen to me. I'm truly not afraid." She caught movement in the corner of her eye—the Protector was approaching. Hastily, she lowered her voice. "I won't surrender to the monster without a fight. My story isn't told yet. Perhaps I can help the island more from outside it than I ever did from its shores. Perhaps we'll yet meet again."

"Ember," her mother moaned. "Ember, you can't—"

"It's time." The Protector's solemn voice cut across whatever warning Ember's mother had been about to give. "I am sorry Hetta, Antoine. The community will be forever grateful for your sacrifice."

Ember noticed that he didn't address thanks to her this time. Like everything else, however, it evoked no reaction within her.

"Right—right now?" gasped her mother. "We don't get any time to say goodbye?"

"There's nothing we need to say, Mother," said Ember in a bracing tone. "We know what we are to each other." She faced the Protector, straightening her back and meeting his eyes boldly. "I'm ready."

Sending each of her parents one more reassuring look, she turned her back on the only community she'd ever known and walked forward to where the Protector waited. As they passed silently through the watching crowd, she felt a surge of determination.

She'd said she didn't want the future planned for her, and she'd been offered a very unexpected means of escape. Everything she'd been told suggested her death was now certain. But yesterday, she'd thought her boring, predictable future on the island was certain. And clearly she'd been wrong. She hadn't even been bold enough to fight that future. Now, she felt galvanized. She would fight the monster with everything she had.

And whatever the outcome, at least she wouldn't have to be a farmer's wife.

The Protector said nothing as he led her out of the silent town. The distance he kept between them would make anyone think she had the plague, Ember reflected. She could probably have run away if she'd tried, but where would she run to? He controlled the whole island. And devastated as her parents might be by her loss, they could never bear the shame of her trying to avoid the role she'd been chosen to play in protecting their island.

Ember glanced behind her as they left the village. No one was in sight. Normally, a spectacle of any kind would bring children trailing behind, to observe the curiosity. Not this time. Everyone was keeping their distance from the condemned girl. Panic curled around the edges of Ember's mind, the atmosphere of fear making it hard to hold on to her determination. But as the island's little wharf drew near, the sight of the tall figure waiting there gave Ember an unexpected surge of courage.

The Protector's brother. Whatever she was feeling, she wasn't going to let him see her fear. It was impossible to shake the suspicion that today's crisis was connected to their encounter the day before, and something deep within Ember refused to let him think he had absolute power over her.

Even if, in reality, he did.

This point was driven home when Ember was ushered into a small boat, and the Protector's brother climbed in after her. The Protector himself said nothing, not even making eye contact as he untied the boat from its mooring.

"Is it just the two of us?" Ember asked, wishing she couldn't hear the nerves in her voice.

By way of answer, he pushed off from the wharf with one oar, deftly steering the boat into deeper water. Too deftly, considering he was no fisherman.

"Wait, shouldn't I have donned the ceremonial gown?" Ember asked suddenly, remembering the last sacrifice, three years earlier.

"It's not necessary," her companion said shortly.

Ember frowned, trying to make sense of this aberration. Perhaps talking would help lift the unbearable tension. "What's the monster like?"

No answer.

"I mean, what does it look like?" she pressed. "What kind of monster is it?"

"We do not speak of it."

The curt answer made her want to roll her eyes. "Surely now, when I'm being imminently sacrificed to it, the situation is a little different. Is it intelligent enough for speech? Will it...eat me? Or just, I don't know...run me through?" A thought occurred to her, and she straightened. "Or might it instead want me to serve it or something?" Hope sprouted in her when her companion didn't immediately answer.

"Is that a possibility?" she said eagerly. If so, she could surely turn it to her advantage. "Maybe I could win its favor.

Maybe I could convince it to stop claiming sacrifices. Or perhaps discover whether we really even still need its protection. I could—"

"This," her companion's cold voice broke into her rambling, "is exactly why you've always been a risk the island cannot afford."

His sure strokes carried them further and further from the shore. A glance back showed the island receding into a shapeless mass.

"This outcome was inevitable," he went on. "It was my brother's weakness to think for so long that you could be dealt with any other way."

Ember frowned. "What does that mean?" she demanded. She gripped the edges of the boat so tightly her knuckles were white. "The selection is supposed to be done by the magic, not by the Protector. How could it be his weakness not to bring about this outcome earlier?"

The man in front of her had fallen silent, but Ember's caution had fled with his words. After all, she had absolutely nothing to lose. She lunged at him, taking advantage of the fact that their seated position evened their heights, and grabbing his collar in both hands.

"What does that mean?" she shouted, her anger unrelated to her own fate. "Are you lying to everyone about the sacrifices?"

The Protector's brother let go of the oars, dropping them into the boat as he seized her hands. He ripped them off his collar with enough force to bruise, flinging her so violently away from him that she fell back into the boat. Ember scrambled upright again, her eyes burning with an anger that was too fierce to allow fear a foothold.

"How dare you touch me?" the man growled. He looked

behind Ember, narrowing his eyes at the now-distant shape of the island. "This is far enough."

"Far enough for what?" Ember demanded, kneeling on the floor of the boat, mentally braced for anything.

By way of answer, her companion slid a blade from his belt. It was slightly curved, the type of blade fishermen used to gut their catches.

"What are you doing?" Ember's eyes fixated on the silver dagger.

"What I've wanted to do for years," he said, his voice dripping with malice.

His movement was sudden as he raised the blade, but Ember was ready. She'd never been as trusting as her peers, ready to always assume the best from their leaders.

She dove out of the way as the blade came flashing down. She dodged the first strike, but there was nowhere to go in the tiny boat, and the second attack was too quick for her to fully avoid. The knife slashed into her leg, and she let out a cry of pain as the man pulled it back out.

There was a gleam in her adversary's eyes, the sight more terrifying even than the blade. He took pleasure from this, from silencing the student who'd constantly questioned him and his empire.

"You're trying to kill me." The words fell from numb lips as a terrible realization crashed over Ember. "You're a singer."

"Me?" No doubt sure of the fight's outcome, her adversary allowed himself to pause his hand as he let out a nasty laugh. "I'm no singer. You are. That's why you can't be allowed to live."

"I'm not a singer!" Ember gasped, fear rippling over her for a reason unrelated to the immediate attack.

It wasn't true. She wasn't born with the capacity to kill in her heart. She couldn't be one of the monsters from their ancestors' stories, the ones who destroyed their homeland.

But a trickle of doubt robbed her words of conviction. She thought of the defiance that bubbled constantly in her, when all her peers seemed content. Was that a sign of a darkness in her heart, one that made her deserving of the death this man was meting out?

No. A surge of clarity came as the Protector's brother once again raised his knife. She wasn't the one with darkness in her heart. She refused to believe she deserved this fate. And she refused to submit to it. She didn't even feel pain in her bleeding leg, the rush of energy that poured through her numbing everything else.

Ember didn't try to dodge out of the way this time. Instead she lunged forward, taking the Protector's brother completely by surprise as she threw her arms around his waist. He'd half-stood in the small space to get more momentum, one foot planted on the floor of the boat and one knee on the narrow bench seat. His balance was thrown off as she charged into him, sending him flying. His blade grazed her shoulder, its sting brief as her attack sent him over the edge of the small vessel, blade still clutched in his hand.

Ember managed to release him at the last moment, barely preventing herself from being pulled into the water as well. The craft rocked crazily, but righted itself in time to avoid filling with water. The Protector's brother had been momentarily submerged, but his head broke the water quickly, a roar of rage sounding from him. Not giving herself time to think, Ember seized the closest oar, gripping it near the flat wooden blade as she brought it smashing down on her opponent's head. He was just reaching for the boat's rim with one hand, but her attack brought his hands up over his head instead. Not hesitating, Ember hit his head twice more with the oar, as hard as she could manage.

She didn't have much strength in her arms—it wasn't enough to knock him out. But he was clearly dazed, his eyes unfocused and his arms flailing in the water as he struggled to keep himself afloat and conscious. Seizing the other oar, Ember lowered both blades into the water and pulled with all her might. She set the sun and the island behind her, rowing frantically westward. Her heart was in her throat with the first few strokes, as the boat moved sluggishly. A cry and a splash behind her told her that the man in the water had come to his senses enough to strike out toward the vessel. But then she hit her stride, and the little craft coasted forward. The next angry cry was far enough behind to embolden her to glance back. He wouldn't be able to catch her now.

"Fool!" he cried, his voice carrying clearly across the water. "You're going the wrong way."

"No, I'm not," she called back, her face set and determined.

His scoff sounded more manic than derisive. "You think yourself a hero? You'll never tell anyone on the island of this. You'll never make it back. The protections will kill you, and good riddance!"

The final words were faint on the wind, and Ember didn't turn again. She suspected he was a strong enough swimmer to make it back to the island, but she didn't let her thoughts dwell on whatever story he'd tell her parents and everyone else. Probably no tale would be necessary. They'd all assume she'd been sacrificed to the monster as planned.

The monster. A trickle of nerves went over Ember as she continued rowing. Was that talk of fatal protections a bluff? Or did it mean the monster was real after all? So much the better if it was real, she told herself firmly. She wasn't going to flee from it. She'd told her mother she wanted a word with this monster, and she'd meant it.

The Protector's brother was far behind now, the island even further. As the sense of immediate crisis faded, her exhaustion rose. Inexperienced in rowing, she didn't have the stamina for such an extended effort. And the pain from her knife wounds was growing rapidly. The shoulder that had sustained the shallow injury burned as she pulled at the oars, and hot agony radiated out from her leg.

Still, Ember refused to slow her pace, keeping the sun firmly at her back as she struck out westward. She'd dreamed all her life of leaving the island and setting out for the mainland. She'd never imagined these circumstances, but a fierce joy still sustained her underneath everything else she was feeling. She'd done it. She was free. And she had a very good reason not to turn back.

Her thoughts swirled irrationally. She would survive this, even if it killed her. She would find the monster, and do all she could do from the mainland to stop the reign of terror that held the island's people captive. Then, she'd return, in spite of what the Protector's brother had said. She'd return and free them from the monsters who hid among them.

How long she'd been rowing before she started to succumb, she couldn't tell. The sun had passed overhead, so it had been some hours. She couldn't guess the exact time, and she was also becoming less sure of her direction. She could only see open water on all sides. She'd paused her efforts to make a clumsy attempt at stemming the flow of blood from her leg wound, but the strip of fabric she'd ripped from her dress and tied around the injury was soaked with blood now. No doubt that was contributing to her growing faintness.

Nothing had occurred to break the monotony of the journey except for a strange sensation some time earlier. For a moment she'd thought it was starting to rain, but the skies remained clear. Whatever had washed over her hadn't been water. It may well have been a product of her over-wrought imagination. Hunger, shock, and exhaustion were wreaking havoc with her mind.

She was aware enough to feel fear as her consciousness started to fade. Adrift on the ocean in this little boat, she'd surely be lost. How would she find her way to the mainland when she woke? If she woke.

Then she saw it. Another vessel in the waters ahead. Ember lowered the oars with shaking arms, waving her hands weakly above her head.

"Help!" she cried, her voice feeble. "Over here."

To her great relief, the other boat, not much larger than hers, changed course. She was too overwhelmed by exhaustion even to worry about whether the strangers were friendly. According to everything she'd been taught, people from the mainland were savage and vengeful. But she'd rather take her chances with them than starve to death while drifting on the ocean.

"Are you all right?" The man who hailed her as the boat drew near looked rough, but his voice wasn't unkind. "Are you all alone out here?"

"I need help," Ember panted. "Please...can you get me to the mainland?" She cast around for something to offer to make them more likely to help her. "You can have this boat in exchange for your help."

The man eyed the little craft with interest. "Looks sturdy enough. But where did you come from?"

Ember ignored the question. "Please. I need to reach land. And I need to find...the monster."

"The monster?" The man raised an eyebrow as his younger companion gave an indulgent chuckle.

"One of those, are ya?" The younger sailor shook his head. "First time I've seen one coming by water. He'll not be too pleased."

"He?" Ember asked, clinging to consciousness with difficulty. Her vision was starting to swim, the dull ache in her leg overwhelming her thoughts.

"Your monster." The man was grinning at her now, revealing a couple of missing teeth.

A thrill of horror washed over Ember, momentarily pushing back her exhaustion. "So it's real?" she whispered. Apparently the Protector's brother hadn't been bluffing. "The monster is real?"

"Aye, real enough," the first man said, more interested in the boat than the conversation, it seemed. "So I can have the boat if I take you to where you can find the monster, eh?"

She nodded, the effort of pulling her head back up way harder than it should have been. "I might need to...regroup before I...challenge him."

"Challenge him." The second man chuckled again. "Aye, he'll like this one."

Ember couldn't tell if he was being sarcastic, but it didn't much matter. She was barely awake as the men pulled her aboard their boat, and the moment her feet hit the wooden floor, she sank into the merciful embrace of unconsciousness.

## CHAPTER FOUR

# Haiden

Haiden bent over the trap, grunting at the catch. A rabbit wasn't what he'd hoped for, but it would be a hot meal that night. Better than more lentils. He reset the trap carefully, ignoring the sight of his hairy, mis-formed hands. They looked like a horrifying mix between human hands and a boar's hooves. Unnatural and highly impractical, if he went by appearances alone.

But in spite of what his eyes told him, his fingers were deft as they worked the delicate contraption that had caught the rabbit for him. The enormous tusks that intruded on his vision barely registered in his mind. After five years, he was well used to the sight. And well aware that when feeling his own face, he would find no trace of them. They were an illusion, nothing more. But an incredibly powerful one.

"Curse that blasted elf and his blasted magic," Haiden muttered bitterly, picking his way through the copse toward his home. A mouse fled before him, no doubt as horrified by the ghastly sight of him as humans were.

Well, most humans. Haiden emerged into the small clearing where he'd built his cottage—himself, stone by stone, without assistance from anyone, thank you very much—and let out a groan. In front of the slightly crooked building stood a slim figure, arrayed in a simple but becoming gown, her fair hair tied back in a braid.

Not another one.

"What do you want?" he growled, making his voice as menacing as possible.

The girl turned, her eyes widening at the sight of him before she made a heroic attempt to school her features. It was a strange sensation, having her fix her eyes so intently at a spot a foot above his head. The illusion made him seem much taller than he was, he'd long since discovered.

"I...I..." The girl's voice came out a squeak, and she swallowed before trying again. "Noble beast, I have traveled far to rescue you from your—"

"Noble beast?" Haiden repeated scornfully. "Is that your idea of a flattering greeting?"

"I...I didn't mean to offend." The girl took an involuntary step backward.

"Then you should have left me alone," Haiden growled. "Get out of here. I'm not a prize for you to claim, and I don't need or want your help."

"But..." The girl's face dropped into a frown, her voice now slightly petulant. "I've come such a long way."

"That's your problem," said Haiden dismissively. "I didn't ask you to come, and I don't want you here."

"But..." The girl looked stumped. "The rumors are that you need the help of a fair maiden to free you from your curse, and then—"

"And then she'll be blessed with wealth and good fortune," Haiden finished in growing irritation. "I've heard the rumors. They're nonsense." He eyed her scornfully. "You probably think I'm some prince in disguise, don't you? Well

I'm not. And for the last time, *I don't want your help.* Now get out of here before I eat you."

He must be losing his touch, because the girl didn't seem daunted by this threat. In fact, she was definitely petulant now. "Aren't you even going to offer me something to eat?" she demanded. "Or a place to stay for the night?"

"Absolutely not!" Haiden said, affronted. "Get off my property."

She eyed him shrewdly. "I'm sure you'll change your mind once you've had something to eat," she said stubbornly. She batted her eyelashes. "I'm an excellent cook." She turned and took a purposeful step toward his cottage.

Not waiting for her to even reach the door and its protective enchantment, Haiden let out a roar, the sound swelling melodically as he pulled magic from the ground. The girl hit an invisible wall, bouncing back comically and rubbing her nose in offense.

"Ow!"

"Do you expect an apology?" Haiden demanded.

She narrowed her eyes at him. "Did you just block me magically from entering? Doesn't that mean you're a singer?"

"What of it?" Haiden swept past her, occupying the doorway to prevent any more attempts at entrance. But he didn't intend to go inside until he'd seen her leave.

"If you're a singer," she pointed out, "why do you even need help lifting your curse? Can't you just do it yourself?"

That was Haiden's limit. Her words stoked his fury, and he let out a roar that was plenty inhuman enough to satisfy any critic.

"GET OUT!"

The girl let out a squeak of real fright, scurrying away with a considerable loss of dignity. Haiden's irritation only grew as he heard her voice raised in a furious reproach the moment she entered the tree line.

"No way, I'm done! He's repulsive AND impossible. I don't want to break his curse and marry him, I don't care how good the reward is!"

Haiden could just make out a low voice arguing angrily back, but he didn't wait to hear the details. He slammed his door, grumbling to himself as he dumped the rabbit on a chair. With unwelcome visitors lingering around, he'd have to wait until later to prepare it.

He wasn't surprised, either by the visit or by whoever hid in the trees. It wasn't the first time he'd seen it. Some of the girls had come on their own initiative, taken with the image of being the one to finally break the local curse after all these years. But others were pushed into it by a father, or brother, or some other enterprising individual looking to benefit from the fabulous reward supposedly attached to the lifting of the curse.

Haiden felt no sympathy for those girls. If they were being used by someone else looking to gain, then they were letting themselves be used. It wasn't his problem that they apparently had no backbone. Besides, he thought cynically, none of them had seemed averse to benefiting on their own behalf.

Haiden stomped around his house, his thoughts angry and detached as he stoked the fire and poured water into a pot. How dare the girl point out that as a singer he should be able to lift his own curse? How dare the idiotic stranger be so...astute?

He tried not to think about the curse, but his memory drew him back to that disastrous day, five years earlier, when he'd tried so rashly to sail for the Reviled Lands.

He knew he'd been very lucky, after he passed out, that

his sails had carried him back to land rather than out into the open ocean. But he didn't feel lucky. And he certainly hadn't been conscious of any sense of good fortune when he'd eventually stormed back into the tavern, demanding to see the elf. He could still hear the screams of terror and see the horror on the faces of the people who'd been present. They'd fled before him like he was a hideous monster, and it had confused him at the time. The pain of the elf's curse—like the pain of hitting the invisible wall of magic that protected the eastern seas—had faded by then. He'd had no idea of the change in his form until the barkeep, with shaking hands, had held up a reflective silver platter in an attempted defense.

Haiden had almost screamed himself at the sight of his horrifying form. At least a foot too tall, his face like an even more hideous version of a boar's, four tusks sprouting from what could only be described as jowls, his whole body covered in coarse brown hair...it wasn't a pleasant sight. And into that moment of pure horror had come a sound that still made his hair prickle in memory.

The elf's snide, malicious laugh.

Haiden had whirled to face him, rage rising up to supplant his fear.

"You!" he cried. "You did this to me!"

The elf grinned nastily. "No. You did it to yourself, like I said you would. I told you that if you tried to run from your destiny, you'd become the monster you fear. You tried to cross the magical barrier on the eastern seas, didn't you? Tried to sail to the Reviled Lands. You must have, since that's what I determined would trigger the curse. I'm impressed you managed to turn back before the barrier killed you."

"I'm not so easily gotten rid of," Haiden growled. "And if

you think I'll meekly beg for you to lift the magic you attacked me with, you can forget it. You won't get that satisfaction."

"Oh, your survival is satisfaction enough for me," the elf said brightly. "I thought you'd likely die in the attempt to cross the barrier, and that would have been such a waste of my magic. The magic could only be triggered by your own actions, you see, since my curse was dependent on you doing what I predicted you would and running from your fears. Crossing the barrier was simply a conveniently concrete way to determine that you'd taken the course I guessed you would." He steepled his fingers in front of him in satisfaction, his expression smug as he looked Haiden's hideous form over. "I'm pleased with the results, I must say. It was a *very* powerful illusion enchantment, and I intended it for other purposes. But I don't begrudge it." His eyes narrowed. "Perhaps now you'll think twice before insulting me or any other elf."

Haiden had started forward with a growl, but the barkeep had been the one to speak.

"All right, elf, you've made your point. Now lift your curse and let the poor boy go."

"I don't think I will," the elf had said placidly.

"I don't want his help," Haiden had snapped. "I don't need it. I'll lift this curse on my own, and be beholden to nobody."

"Don't be foolish, lad," the barkeep had said impatiently. "You can't go around like that. You'll get yourself killed, or hurt someone."

"Stay out of it," Haiden had growled, his anger getting the better of his good sense. If he'd had any of that back then.

"You should listen." He could still see the elf's smirk.

"You won't be able to break this one yourself. When I released it, I molded it just for you. If you want to be free of the curse, you'll have to depend on someone else for help. You'll have to actually *ask* them." His eyes glinted. "Aren't you going to ask me now? Go ahead."

"Never." Haiden's own growl reverberated in his head, all these years later.

He hadn't meant it, though. He'd thought he had, in the moment. But his resolve had failed him. He'd lasted almost a year of misery and isolation and futile attempts to use his own magic to lift the curse before crawling back to the elf.

Asking for help had been the most bitter experience of his life. Made more bitter by the elf's response.

"No, I don't think so." The diminutive creature's grin was etched on Haiden's memory. "I don't feel inclined to use my limited magic that way."

"You said," Haiden had growled through gritted teeth, "that I had to ask for help."

"Yes, I did," the elf agreed. "You have to ask. But it should be obvious that the person you ask has to be both capable of helping you and willing to do it." He sniffed. "Which I am not. Good luck."

And that had been the last Haiden had seen of the elf. In the more than four years that had passed, he'd never once entertained the idea of trying again to ask the vile creature for help. He'd gone against his instincts one time, and he'd well and truly learned his lesson. There would be no point—this elf was truly a rogue, an outcast from his own kind. He hadn't even tried to strike a bargain with Haiden in exchange for the help sought, as any self-respecting elf would do. He clearly just wanted to inflict suffering on the human who'd dared to insult him and accurately guess the reason for his isolation.

But it didn't matter that the vindictive creature wouldn't help. Whatever the elf said, Haiden *would* get out of this curse on his own. He'd thought more than once about asking his sister for help. But he'd left Terenford for the sole reason of finding his way in life out of Gisela's shadow. He simply couldn't bear to crawl back there in his current state, meekly admitting he couldn't survive in the world without her. Not to mention she didn't deserve to have him bring trouble on her doorstep. She was royal now, and had much bigger things to worry about than her reckless brother. Five years wasn't enough to break his spirits—he wasn't yet that desperate.

He glanced toward the door of his cottage, his lips curling in a sneer. He certainly wouldn't be looking for help from fools like that girl or her companion. It seemed likely that the elf was responsible for the ridiculous rumors that had brought a steady trickle of maddening intruders into Haiden's clearing. He didn't doubt the creature was keeping an eye on him from somewhere not too far away.

Gloating.

The thought made Haiden grit his teeth, but he didn't let himself give in to the rage. He'd done that far too many times, and it didn't lead to anything productive.

When he was confident he was alone, Haiden emerged from his cottage and set about preparing his catch. The light was fading as he sang softly to himself, testing the enchantments around the cottage. Perhaps he should expand them to keep people out of the clearing altogether. It was probably a waste of his magical resources. He should be focusing all his efforts on breaking his curse so he could continue with his original plan.

Because whatever anyone in the village said, he still fully intended to reach the Reviled Lands. He'd come east looking for answers, and no hairy boar-faced illusion was going to keep him from finding them. It was just an unplanned diversion, and all journeys were full of those.

The evening was mild, and Haiden decided to cook his rabbit over his outdoor fire. He was therefore perfectly able to hear the telltale cracking of a twig just as the stars were coming out.

"Who is it?" he growled into the darkness. "Stay out of my clearing, whoever you are. I'm not interested in your company."

There was a moment of stillness, then a form emerged from the tree line. Haiden let out a groan at the sight of yet another unaccompanied young woman. Two in one day? That was unusually bad. Would he never be rid of them?

"So you can speak, can you?" The girl held herself haughtily, although her voice shook slightly. "That's more than I bargained for."

"I don't care what you bargained for," said Haiden, affronted by this greeting. Was that how she thought to win him over and break his curse? "I told you, I'm not interested in your company."

Most unexpectedly, the girl let out a snort. With one agitated hand, she swept a mass of curly red hair out of her eyes. "Did it occur to you that I don't care what you're interested in?"

Her gesture made Haiden properly look at her for the first time. She didn't have the look of the other girls at all. Usually, they were becomingly attired and well presented, clearly hoping to impress the beast with their beauty.

Idiots.

This girl was...a complete mess. Her hair was a riot of tangles, her face drawn with dark shadows under her eyes, and her dress ripped and dirty.

A damsel in need of his help? Haiden scowled. That was even worse than a damsel trying to help him. In fact, he realized, it was probably the same thing. Some ruse, no doubt.

"Let me say it more clearly," he said, his voice a low and dangerous rumble. "Get off my land before I drive you off in a manner you won't like."

She gave a laugh that bordered on hysterical. "I realize you don't know anything about me or what I've been through to get here, but even so...did you really think that would be enough to scare me?"

His patience abruptly running out, Haiden pushed himself to his feet. He saw her eyes follow the movement, their expression wary as they rested on a spot a foot above his head, but not filled with terror. Come to think of it, even at first sight of him, she'd shown none of the fear and horror he'd come to expect from new acquaintances.

"So I don't scare you?" he asked, injecting as much menace into his voice as he could manage. "Not at all?"

She straightened even further, taking a step forward rather than retreating. Haiden noticed the limp that accompanied the movement, and was taken aback to realize that one side of her gown was stained with blood. He'd failed to notice in the firelight. What exactly was this waif's story?

"No, I'm not," she said evenly. "If you want the truth, you're pathetically tame compared to the monster I was expecting. And—I'm inclined to think—your obviously vile appearance makes you *less* terrifying than the monsters I left behind."

None of that speech made any sense to Haiden, and he had no interest in getting to the bottom of it.

"Well, I'm glad your curiosity has been satisfied," he said

waspishly. "Now that you've seen the spectacle, you can leave me alone."

"My curiosity has *not* been satisfied!" She stamped her foot like a petulant child, then instantly regretted it, judging by the wince that crossed her face. It was swiftly replaced with a scowl she no doubt intended to be menacing. "I want to know what's become of the others."

"Others?" Haiden asked, nonplussed.

"The other girls!" she said, her temper rising. "The innocent maidens who came before me."

"I don't know or care what became of them," said Haiden, irked. "They're not my responsibility."

"Not your responsibility?" the stranger demanded angrily. "Have you no shame?"

"None whatsoever," Haiden said promptly.

"Are they alive?" she said, growing more agitated. "Surely you can tell me that much."

"No, I can't." Haiden matched her scowl. "I told you, I don't know or care what became of any of them."

"Well, I care!"

She was visibly shaking now, and Haiden found himself watching in a kind of detached fascination as she took another step toward him. She was the oddest maiden rescuer who'd ever intruded on his peace.

Unfortunately, her entertaining tirade was cut short. With the next stride, the girl quite suddenly collapsed. It was as though her leg refused to support her weight, and her body crumpled before Haiden's eyes like a rag doll's.

"Hello?" He said the word gruffly, irritation still his primary emotion. "Oi. Get up."

He stepped warily up to her and nudged her still form with his hoof-like foot. Peering down, he saw that her chest rose and fell, so it appeared she wasn't dead. Was this another ploy? Part of the act? No doubt she hoped to be taken inside to recover from...whatever malady had made her look like a drowned rat.

Haiden let out a huff. He wasn't so easily manipulated. Turning his back on the girl, he strode into his cottage and slammed the door. It was several minutes before he remembered his rabbit, still strung over the fire. He let out a groan. Going back out there was surely what the girl wanted him to do. But he was hungry, and the rabbit would burn if he didn't get it soon.

Resentfully, he marched back out, resolving to ignore the girl altogether. But he couldn't stop his eyes darting to her as he salvaged his dinner. Her hair was a fiery mass over her face, leaving only one eye and the corner of her lips exposed. There was no sign of consciousness there.

Cursing his own softness, Haiden approached her. With one foot, he rolled her over, hoping to study her face for a better clue as to whether she was faking it. But all he achieved was for her hair to cover her whole face. With a sigh, he squatted beside her, reaching out a hand to shift the red curls. His eyes saw the coarse hair of the boar-man, but his fingers felt human and capable as he flicked her hair from her face. Her skin was cool under his touch, not warm like a human cheek should be. Haiden searched her features carefully, looking for any sign that she was aware she'd caught his interest.

He straightened, frowning. What did it matter if she was faking? Even if she wasn't, it didn't mean it wasn't a ploy. Even if it *wasn't* a ploy, did that change anything? He wanted to be left alone, and he had no responsibility for whatever disaster had befallen this total stranger. What right did she have to expect him to help her?

Even in his thoughts, Haiden recognized how petulant

his voice sounded. He was annoyed because he knew his arguments were futile. He'd already decided to help her. He was angry with himself for being weak and gullible, and angry with her for placing him in that situation. But it didn't change the fact that monster though he might be, he apparently wasn't capable of leaving this girl alone in the night, bleeding and unconscious and cold.

Resentment simmering angrily within him, he hoisted her into his arms and strode toward the cottage.

## CHAPTER FIVE

# Ember

Consciousness returned to Ember with a jolt, and she drew in a breath that was closer to a gasp. It felt like the first breath of air after being underwater. In fact, she had a feeling she might have been dreaming about drowning.

But she wasn't underwater now, and she wasn't dreaming. She was warm and dry. Slowly, she opened her eyes to see a simple building, bare stone walls pressing close around her, no decorations or furnishings of any kind. The room held a small cupboard and kitchen bench, but very little else. She was laid down on a pallet mattress, not nearly as comfortable as her bed at home on the island. In fact, the whole place was nothing like home. Her family's dwelling had been humble, but it had been neat and well-made. Not to mention tidy.

"That masonry isn't even at all," she commented aloud to no one in particular.

"Thank you for your feedback."

The irritable voice brought her sitting bolt upright, memory returning in a rush. Her eyes widened as they rested on the revolting creature before her, standing framed in the doorway that led outside. What *was* he? If she had to describe him, she'd say half-human, half-boar. But that didn't fully capture the...*wrongness* of his form.

"What did you do to me?" she demanded, uneasy to realize that she'd been completely in his power. "Why did you bring me into your home?"

He snorted, the sound very human in spite of his hog-like snout and protruding tusks. "I didn't do it gladly. That's the gratitude I get, is it?"

"Gratitude?!" Ember protested, pushing herself to a standing position. Her leg swayed beneath her, the dull ache from the day before reasserting itself. "You expect gratitude after what you've done? Did the others try to flatter you to beg for survival? I won't."

The monster looked her over with clear disdain. "I have no idea why you would."

She narrowed her eyes at him. "I mean it," she said. "I'm not going to beg, or scream, or run. If you're going to kill me, just do it now. You won't get anything else from me."

"If I was going to kill you," he said acidly, "don't you think I would have done it when you were unconscious?"

"Not necessarily," Ember said. "Not if you get some kind of sick satisfaction from seeing others' fear, or chasing down your prey. Then it would be very boring if I was unconscious."

"True," he acknowledged, apparently struck by this perspective. "But I hardly think I would have bothered to bind your wounds in that case."

Frowning in confusion, Ember glanced down at herself. She was still in her ripped, blood-stained gown, but now she was paying attention, her leg felt much more secure. She flicked the skirts aside, surprised to see a clean bandage wrapped firmly around the knife wound inflicted by the Protector's brother. Even her shoulder had a plaster attached to it.

"Why did you do that?" she demanded, unnerved. She studied him carefully, but any emotions he felt were impossible to discern on that ridiculous boar face. "I can't see what motivation you have for demanding innocent maidens if you don't take pleasure from killing them."

Again, the creature snorted. "Demanding? You think I ask for these girls to come to me? You think I *want* them intruding?"

Ember felt the color drain from her face as she took in his words—even she hadn't guessed that the Protector's treachery went this deep.

"You mean...you don't ask for them? For us? They're sent without you even wanting them?"

"Obviously." The creature sounded bored now.

"But what do you do with them?" she demanded. She frowned. "And how old are you, anyway? *What* are you?"

"Not a very polite question," he pointed out.

She waved this criticism aside impatiently. "I'm serious. You speak and move like a human, but you look like..." She waved an expressive hand. "Whatever chaos that is. But girls have been sacrificed every five years for three decades. How long have you been doing...whatever it is you're doing?"

This time she could read his bewilderment even on his unnatural features. It was the eyes, she realized. On closer inspection, they were very much human.

"Every five years? The last girl before you came yesterday afternoon. And they haven't been coming for three decades. I've only been here for five years." He shook his head, his boar-like ears standing up stiff. "The rumors grow more absurd with every retelling." Those human eyes narrowed as they stared at her. "And you're obviously an imbecile to believe them. I don't have the patience to explain how the world works to you. You're patched up, and you're conscious. Now get out of here and leave me in peace."

"I don't think so," Ember said flatly. She was unconvinced by his weak excuses. If he had girls coming to him more frequently than the island was sending them, he must be terrorizing other communities as well as hers. And wherever he'd been before five years ago, it couldn't have been far from the coast, since she knew for certain girls had been sent for longer than five years. "I'm not leaving without answers."

"Yes, you are." The creature strode toward her, reaching out one weirdly hoof-like hand toward her. He gripped her uninjured shoulder with painful force, causing Ember to stare down at it in surprise.

"If you don't want to get hurt, don't force yourself into the home of a monster," said the creature shortly, obviously irked by her expression.

"I didn't force myself in here," she pointed out. "You carried me in while I was unconscious."

What she didn't say was that her surprise had nothing to do with the roughness of his hold. It came from the feel of it. Her eyes saw coarse hair and hoof-like fingers. But she didn't feel any of that. She felt the grip of a hand that seemed completely...human.

"What are you?" she asked again.

"A monster." The reply was terse as he started to shove her toward the door. "Now get out of my house."

"I don't think I will," Ember said, boldly pushing his hand off. Again, she felt skin that, while not exactly soft, had all the smoothness of human fingers. Since he clearly didn't like being asked what he was, she opted for a more polite approach. "What's your name?"

He hesitated for so long she thought he wouldn't answer. When he did so, his voice was gruff.

"Haiden."

"Haiden?" She couldn't help the bubble of amusement that rose inside her.

Apparently he didn't appreciate that either. "Something funny about my name?"

"Not in itself," she said. "It's just...not a very good name for a monster. I was expecting something a little more fierce."

"If you want fierce," he started irritably, "I can rise to the occasion."

"No, stop trying to intimidate me." She waved him off distractedly. "You're not nearly as good at it as you think, not when you're trying it on someone who's grown up believing you to be an all-powerful, terrifying monster who eats damsels for breakfast."

"*Grown up* believing...?" He trailed off. "What in the blazes are you talking about?"

Ember ignored him. "My name is Ember, by the way. And since you're clearly not going to eat me, I've decided you're going to help me instead."

"Help you—?" He didn't need human features to communicate his outrage. It was clear in his voice. "Listen here, *wench*, I don't know or care who you are or what your problems are. I have no intention of helping you with anything, and I most definitely don't want your help."

"My help?" Ember repeated, surprised. "I didn't offer you my help. And I'm not likely to. You have plenty to answer for, even if rumors have exaggerated the true situation." She squinted at him. "Also, what does *wench* mean?"

He let out a long, gravelly breath.

"What?" she pressed. "Is it supposed to be insulting?"

"Can you just get out of my house now?" he asked.

"Why?" she asked, intrigued by his refusal to answer. "Is it something so terrible? Would your mother be ashamed of you?" She paused. "Do you *have* a mother?"

He let out a snort. "Sort of," he said. "And she's already much worse than ashamed of me, so I don't think me calling you wench would tip the balance much."

"So why won't you explain?" she demanded.

He made an irritated noise in the back of his throat. "Because insulting someone isn't at all satisfying if you have to explain the insult."

Ember tilted her head to one side, considering this. After a long moment, she nodded slowly. "Yes," she acknowledged. "I can see that."

She almost thought she saw his mouth twitch, but it might have been some boar instinct rather than humor.

"So why is your mother ashamed of you?" she asked, seating herself back on the bed. "Is it because you're a boar-man-thing?"

"No." He tapped one hoofed foot impatiently, his arms crossed. "Enough questions. It's time for you to leave."

"Yes, I wouldn't mind leaving the house," she said amicably, strolling past him and through the doorway. She lifted her face to the sky. "Fresh air is what I need. I didn't make it all the way to the mainland to sit inside these four poorly built walls." She turned back to face him. "But I'm not *leaving* leaving. I'm staying here until you help me."

"I'm not helping you," Haiden said angrily. "Now get out of my clearing."

With that, he slammed the door, leaving Ember blinking at it. Her stomach gave a rumble, reminding her how long it had been since the fishermen to whom she'd given her boat had shared some bread with her.

"Could have at least offered me some food," she muttered resentfully.

"NO! Get your own food!" The answering shout made her jump, then grin. Apparently he wasn't quite as capable of ignoring the intruder as he wanted to seem.

Not easily discouraged, Ember made for the door again. But the moment she touched the handle, she found her hand thrown backward, a painful jolt passing into her body for good measure.

"Interesting," she murmured, turning her hand over as the pain receded. "That seems like magic." Far from being deterred by the protection, she felt elated. Clearly there was magic on the mainland, as one would imagine in a land of monsters. And if it could be used for little details like keeping unwanted visitors from opening your door, it was presumably more plentiful than the magic of the island, which mainly just served to guide the leaders on important decisions.

Ember didn't try the door again, deciding that there was a time to push her way in, and a time to be patient. She seated herself on a log. If she ignored her hunger, she was quite content. She'd achieved what she'd dreamed of all her life, making it off the island and finding the mainland. The whole world was suddenly before her, and she felt a sense of calm—of *rightness*—she never had before. Everything felt different. Something in her could sense that this land went for miles and miles, for day upon day of travel. It was full of places, landscapes, people the island didn't hold.

And she was alive! Such a short time before, she'd thought herself sentenced to be sacrificed. Now she'd found that the monster was nothing like the specter of death she'd been led to believe. Honestly, he was more like a sulky child hiding his ill temper behind a scary mask. If anything, it was embarrassing that her leaders sought his protection and her people lived in fear of him. His world certainly didn't seem like a place they urgently needed to be protected from.

But that thought sobered her. The island did need protecting, just not from the monster on the mainland. From the monsters in their midst. Not to mention that her parents were no doubt devastated by the grief of her supposed death. She couldn't leave them to suffer.

She sat with her thoughts for at least an hour, until the sun appeared over the tops of the trees and shone warmly down into the little clearing. When the door to the cottage opened again, she turned with a bright smile, having decided she would have more success if she didn't antagonize Haiden further.

"What are you still doing here?"

The growl didn't trouble Ember. He didn't sound surprised—no doubt he'd seen her out the window before emerging.

"Waiting for you," she said cheerfully. She noted the ax in his hand. "Going for a walk? I'll join."

"No, you won't," he said, irked. "Why is it so hard for you to get it through your thick head? I want to be left alone."

"Well, we can't always have what we want," Ember informed him sagely. "For example, I want your help, you want me to go away." She blinked innocently up at his ghastly face. "Only one of us is going to get what we want, aren't we?"

He narrowed those human eyes at her, and she kept her expression bland, daring him to test her resolve. Because she was resolved. She'd reached a conclusion during her pondering. Much as she might want to set off to explore the mainland, it would be unforgivably selfish. Her priority had to be freeing her island home from the lies that held it captive.

Apparently Haiden decided not to engage with her challenge. Shouldering his ax, he turned away and strode into the trees. Ember skipped along after him, looking around her with interest.

"What's the ax for?" she asked. "Chopping up firewood?"

"Killing you and burying you in the woods," he replied.

She chuckled. "The ax won't be much use in burying me."

A grunt was his only reply.

They walked on in silence for a few minutes, Haiden pausing occasionally to check well-hidden traps. The first two were empty.

"What did you mean before?" he asked abruptly, as they navigated their way through the undergrowth.

"Which part?" Ember asked, her eyes on a nest above them.

"You said something about making it all the way to the mainland." Haiden seemed to resent betraying interest in her tale.

"Oh, that." Ember paused, confused as to why the monster, of all individuals, would need an explanation. "Obviously I wasn't born here," she said. "Wherever here is."

Haiden stopped walking, his tusked head swiveling to face her. "You don't know what kingdom you're in?"

Ember shook her head.

He frowned at her for a long moment before giving a gruff reply. "You're in the kingdom of Vadolis. Specifically, the eastern coast. It's the easternmost of the four kingdoms that make up Providore's mainland."

She nodded. "Thank you. That's helpful." She paused, before adding delicately, "So Providore is the name of the mainland?"

"Where are you from?" Haiden demanded, turning fully to face her. "How is it that you don't even know the name of the continent?"

"You know where I'm from," Ember said impatiently. "You've got a deal with the leaders of my island. You're the one who protects us from discovery. I really can't see how it benefits you to play dumb."

"I've never played dumb in my life," Haiden said in irritation. "And I have no idea what you're talking about. I don't have any deal with the leaders of any island."

Ember frowned, holding herself tensely as she tried to decide how to reply. In spite of her flippant demeanor, she was vividly aware of the ax in the boar-man's hand. She couldn't guess what game he was playing, or what the consequences of a misstep might be for her. But as she studied him, she had to admit that he really did seem perplexed, in his angry, impatient way. Was it possible he was telling the truth?

"Are...are there any other monsters around here?" she asked delicately.

Haiden snorted. "Not that I've ever heard of. It's just me."

Ember bit her lip, unnerved by this information and still confused about his intentions in claiming ignorance. Perhaps she'd be wisest to continue as if taking all his words at face value. Working on the assumption that he really didn't know about the island, he would need to know if she was going to convince him—or trick him, or manipulate him, or whatever—into helping her.

"I'm from an island," she blurted out. "It's east of here. It's not very big, but it's fully self-contained. My people have lived there for generations, and no one ever leaves."

Haiden considered her silently. "No one?"

"Except...except me," Ember amended lamely.

"How long did it take you to get from your island to here?" Haiden asked.

Ember fiddled with the torn folds of her gown. "I don't know, exactly," she admitted. "I spent a fair chunk of the voyage passed out in the bottom of some fisherman's boat. But I think it was more than one whole day, less than two?"

Haiden's face was impossible to read, but something in his voice told her she finally had his full attention. "So...so you're not from the Reviled Lands?"

She frowned, feeling wary. "The Reviled Lands? I don't know where that is."

"It's the smaller continent east of Providore," Haiden said. "It's been cut off for generations, because of some kind of internal war that happened over there. A war that made the kingdoms of Providore want nothing to do with them. But it's further east than what you're describing. And it's not a small island. At least, not as far as I understand. No one knows much about it."

"Oh." Ember couldn't think what else to say, her heart racing uncomfortably. He was obviously speaking of her ancestors' homeland. She needed to tread very carefully.

"If that's where you're really from," his gruff voice sounded the closest to gentle that she'd ever heard it, "you can tell me the truth. You don't need to be afraid."

"I don't?" she quipped, his softer manner only making her

more unnerved. "I thought you were going to kill me with that ax and bury me in the woods." She saw that he looked unimpressed again, and added for good measure, "And I'm not from these Reviled Lands. I'm from a small island, like I said."

"Hm."

Haiden didn't seem convinced, but he didn't press the point. Instead, he turned away, shifting the ax in its position over his shoulder. Ember let out a long breath, feeling as though she'd successfully navigated an unknown danger. At least for now.

A sweet sound cut through the air, and Ember lifted her face, enchanted. "What's that lovely call? I don't recognize it."

"It's a thrush," said Haiden, moving forward again.

Ember followed, her eyes still searching the canopy above.

"Personally I don't think they're anything special compared to the birds in the forest where I grew up," Haiden added. "But around here, everyone seems to think they have a beautiful song."

"What?" Something in her voice made Haiden stop, turning to look at her. His eyes narrowed in confusion as he took in her expression. Shock was rippling over her, and she had no doubt she'd gone pale. "What did you just say?"

"Everyone thinks the thrush sounds beautiful," Haiden repeated. "But I don't care for its song that much."

Ember swallowed, forcing the words out through numb lips. "Its...its song?"

## CHAPTER SIX

# Ember

Haiden continued to stare at Ember like he thought she'd lost her mind. She was feeling a little that way herself.

"What are you, a bird fanatic?" he asked dryly. "Are you so offended that I don't love the thrush's song?"

"What do you mean by the bird's...song?" Ember asked in hushed tones.

"I mean exactly that." Haiden was still staring at her. "That's what it's called. Birdsong."

"No, it's not," she contradicted, unwilling to say the word again. It was strange to hear him say it so casually. It felt like using dirty language. "It's birdcall."

"What exactly do you think birdcall is?" Haiden said, clearly impatient with the conversation.

"You know...that." She gestured vaguely upward to indicate the still-active thrush. "How birds' voices sound. Like this." Once again gripped by that inexplicable urge, she raised her own voice in attempted imitation of the bird.

Haiden stilled, staring at her with more intensity than ever.

"Do that again," he said quietly.

Ember shut her mouth with a snap, fear pouring over her. What had possessed her to do that? How had she let herself get caught up in the impulse and forget the response of the last person to witness that trick?

But apparently Haiden didn't need her to repeat the performance to draw the worst kind of conclusion.

"You're a singer," he said simply. "But a very inexperienced one, apparently."

"I...I'm not a singer," said Ember, wishing she sounded more confident of it. She remembered the words of the Protector's brother after he'd stabbed her in the boat.

*I'm no singer. You are. That's why you can't be allowed to live.*

It couldn't be true. She refused to believe it.

"Of course you are," Haiden said impatiently. "Do you think I can't tell?"

"You're lying!" The words burst from Ember with a passion that obviously surprised Haiden. "I'm no more a singer than that bird."

He stared from her to the treetops where the thrush was hidden. "Birds can't be singers," he said, like he was talking to a small child. "They can't learn songcraft. Even the select few humans who can have to be taught to use their ability properly. Do you really not know any of this?"

"Taught?" Ember gasped. "Why would anyone teach someone else how to sing?"

Haiden lowered his ax, resting it on the ground and leaning on the handle. "Because," he said, as if it was obvious, "no singer can reach his or her potential without training."

"Potential?" Ember whispered. It was chilling to hear

him speak of the ability to kill as promising potential. Was the mainland as brutal as she'd been taught after all?

"Yes, potential." Haiden still spoke with exaggerated slowness, his tone definitely an insult to her intelligence. "Every kingdom has an Academy of Song to develop the talent of singers born within its borders. I attended one myself for two years."

The quiet forest seemed to spin around Ember. She stumbled back a step in horror.

"You...you're a singer?"

"Yes, I'm a singer." Haiden's eyes narrowed as he took in her expression. "Do you have a problem with that?"

"How could anyone not?" Ember gasped through numb lips. She was aghast that he could admit it so brazenly.

"So this form doesn't bother you, but the fact that I'm a singer does?" Haiden's anger was growing.

Ember swallowed, words failing her. She'd begun to think he wasn't a true monster, but a cursed human. And if he was a singer—something only humans could be—it must be true. But that only made it worse.

"You can get off your high horse, Ember," Haiden said her name with insulting emphasis, "because if I'm a monster, so are you."

"I'm *not* a singer," she said hotly.

"You are." Haiden's tone was dismissive now. "And denying it won't change a thing. You were born with songcraft in your blood, and you'll carry it until you die. You can't outrun it. Believe me, I know."

"You're wrong." Ember's hands shook, and she balled them into fists in her skirts in an effort to still them. "And I don't want or need help from a monster like you. I'll save my island without you."

"Good!" said Haiden angrily. "Finally we're in agreement!"

"Good!" Ember echoed. "Just point me to the closest village, and I'll never trouble you again."

"Finally." Haiden's glower didn't match his words, but he raised one hair-covered arm to point through the trees. "Arville is south. That way."

Ember didn't thank him. She turned abruptly, striding blindly between the trunks. Whatever was going on with this strange boar-man in his hermit cottage, born with the capacity to kill but apparently disinclined to kill her in particular, she wanted no part of it.

She was fortunate that the forest didn't continue much longer after the point where she'd left Haiden. By the time she emerged from the trees, she wasn't confident she was still going the right direction. But a small rise in the ground allowed her a view of the area, including the coastline and the sparkling sea beyond. She positioned it on her left and kept moving south.

It only took about an hour of brisk walking to bring a village into view. By that time, Ember was exhausted, her weakened state exacerbated by her hunger and her injuries. She was miserably aware that she was vulnerable to anyone who might wish her harm, and her survival was likely dependent on some stranger being willing to offer her help.

And how would she know which strangers to trust? She couldn't even tell a murderer from a like-minded spirit.

That was the part that unnerved her most, she realized. In spite of his rudeness, in spite of what she'd been led to expect, she'd warmed to him. There was a restless spirit about him that had been familiar enough to be endearing.

And all the time, he'd been a born murderer, and she'd been too naive to recognize it.

"Come on, Ember," she muttered to herself, as she passed between the first outlying buildings of the village. "The boar face didn't give you a clue?"

She knew as she made her way into the village that she wasn't going to blend in. Even in her own island marketplace, she'd stood out merely for attending on the wrong day. Here, known to no one, she would be marked from the moment she met another human.

The thought was depressing. Ember had often felt alone back on her island, with no one able to understand her longing for a different life. But it was nothing to the true isolation she experienced as stranger after stranger stared at her as she passed, with expressions ranging from curious to calculating. She surprised herself by feeling a bizarre urge to turn and flee back to Haiden's clearing.

*You'd rather spend time with a half-beast killer than your own kind?*

The reproachful voice in her head galvanized her, and she pushed on into the village. The people around her were at least human, and she shouldn't assume without meeting them that they were savage or unfriendly.

"Excuse me," she said, gathering her courage and approaching a matronly looking woman. "Do you know where I can find some food?"

The woman looked her over, her gaze lingering on the large bloodstain on Ember's skirts. "The tavern's over there," she said, pointing to a building that was slightly larger than those around it. "Barkeep might be in a good mood, and let you in even in that state."

"Thank you," said Ember meekly. At least she knew what a tavern was. The island had one, a clean and pleasant meeting place for men after a hard day's work. Her father had taken her in there once or twice to pass on a message or return a borrowed item.

The moment Ember stepped into Arville's tavern, however, it became clear that it was a different sort of establishment. It was darker than the one on the island, there was an unfamiliar smell in the air, and some of the patrons looked the worse for wear. Ember swallowed nervously as every eye flew to her in the doorway, a pair of men muttering behind their tankards.

But it was no good turning back, because she had nowhere else to go. Holding her head high, Ember walked up to the bar, trying to inject confidence in her voice as the barkeep fixed her with the same scrutiny as everyone else in the room.

"Good afternoon," she said. "I was told that I might find food here."

"Aye," the barkeep said noncommittally. "If you've the coins to pay for it."

Ember felt her upright posture tremble a little. "Coins?"

"Yes, coins," he said, raising an eyebrow.

Ember bit her lip, deciding not to admit that she didn't know what coins were. "I...I don't have any coins on me...at present."

"Then I'm not sure what you think I can do for you," the barkeep said.

"Ah, go easy." A new voice entered the conversation, a broad-shouldered man leaving his seat to stroll up to the bar. His dark hair was streaked with gray, and he looked weathered from years in the sun. It occurred to Ember that he had the feel of a middle-aged version of Gil. "The poor girl looks like she's been through fire." He gave Ember a searching look. "Are you all right, lass?"

She swallowed, the unexpected kindness almost enough to make her burst into tears.

"I've been better," she acknowledged.

"Where have you come from?" he asked.

Ember's mind raced. She didn't think it would be a good idea to tell this room full of strangers about the island. But she had to say somewhere. They obviously knew she wasn't from this village.

"I...I've just walked from a nearby cottage," she said. "North of here. In a clearing where—"

"Ah." The man interrupted her with a sigh. "Don't tell me you're another one of these girls coming through in hopes of breaking the monster's curse."

"No," said Ember, more confused than ever about Haiden's situation, but disgruntled by the suggestion nonetheless. "I didn't go there to help him."

Neither the kindly man nor the barkeep looked convinced.

"We've another upstairs," the barkeep said. "So don't think you'll make yourself a spectacle if you own up to it."

"Another what?" Ember demanded, nonplussed.

"Another girl who came here to try to break the curse. Came back in a foul temper, too, so I don't think her efforts yielded much."

Ember stared at him. Was that who Haiden had been speaking about when he said the last girl came only the previous afternoon? Apparently he hadn't killed that girl, then, as she'd imagined when he admitted to being a born murderer.

"I told you," Ember said more cautiously, aware that she didn't have all the information, "I have no intention of helping that...creature."

The barkeep raised an eyebrow. "Worse than you expected, was he?"

An exaggerated sniff from next to the bar made them all look over to see a girl with sleek blond hair pulled back into a braid. A young man stood beside her, his features similar to hers.

"He was certainly hideous, you're not wrong," the girl said. "And his manners were even worse than his appearance."

Ember eyed her with disfavor. "It wasn't his appearance that troubled me. Or his manners. It's that he's a...singer." Her voice dropped on the last word. "And not even ashamed of it."

The girl raised an eyebrow, her expression more condescending than ever. "Yes, I discovered that, too. You'd think he'd be able to help himself out of the mess he's in, wouldn't you?"

"Why would he be ashamed of being a singer?" the friendly man asked Ember in bewilderment. "Where do you come from that singers are so reviled?"

The word *reviled* made Ember pause, reminding her of the name Haiden had given her ancestors' homeland—the Reviled Lands. But it just made their reaction all the more puzzling—those lands were reviled because they'd been overthrown by singers.

"I don't understand," she said cautiously. "Why would anyone *not* be ashamed of being a singer?"

The middle-aged Gil frowned, resting one elbow on the bar and leaning on it.

"What do you think a singer *does*, lass?"

"Well...kills people," said Ember. "Singing is the ability to kill other humans."

A guffaw sounded from the fair-haired girl. "You're

adorable," she told Ember. "A real rustic. What cave did you grow up in that you don't even know what singing is?"

Ember bristled. "Since you apparently know everything," she said sweetly, "why don't you correct me?"

The girl rolled her eyes. "Why don't you go ask the monster? Since you were so taken with his appearance and manners."

Before Ember could retort, the kindly man intervened.

"That's not what singers are, child. Singers are those born with the ability to release song with their voices. When they do that, they draw magic up from the ground and sort of channel it." He shrugged. "I don't know how it all works. But they usually go to special schools to study how to use their magic properly. They can do all kinds of incredible things if they're trained. I once saw a singer mend a ripped garment with nothing but his voice."

For a long moment, Ember just stared at him, feeling more foolish than she ever had in her life.

"That...that can't be true," she said stupidly. That couldn't be what singing really meant.

"She really didn't know!" crowed the other girl, letting out a peal of laughter that grated on Ember's ears.

Ember ignored her, keeping her eyes fixed on the man who'd explained it without ridiculing her. "So singers truly aren't killers?"

He shrugged again. "Not by definition. Some might be, I suppose. Same as anyone. And I have no doubt there are ways to use magic to kill someone, if a singer was so inclined. But singing in itself has nothing to do with killing." He narrowed his eyes shrewdly as he studied her. "Where are you from, where they taught you such a twisted version of what magic is?"

Ember just gave her head a little shake, too overwhelmed for speech even if she had been willing to share her origins. One glance around the tavern was enough to convince her he wasn't lying. His explanation was clearly the most commonplace information that everyone present had known all their lives.

The man had asked who'd given her such a twisted view of magic. But back on the island, they didn't connect singing with magic. Singing was the murderous aberration that had caused some among their ancestors to rise up and destroy their old homeland. Magic was something else entirely, something that came from the island itself and guided their leaders. Something that gave them authority and reinforced their decisions.

Or so they'd claimed. Just how deep did their lies go?

"Are you all right, lass?" the stranger asked gently.

"Not really." Ember had no energy for deception. But of course these people could have no concept of how dramatically they'd just shattered her world.

"Can't you give her some food, and a place to sleep?" the man asked the barkeep.

He frowned. "I'm not running a charity. She says she has no coins."

"Are coins the only payment you accept?" Ember asked, pulling herself together and taking a hand in the conversation. It was a shame that she had no regal onyx, but who knew if they'd even accept that as currency on the mainland? "Back home, we sometimes trade for goods and labor and the like." She glanced around the tavern. "I can cook and clean. Isn't there any work you need done that could earn a meal and one night's stay?"

The barkeep gave her a long and contemplative look before letting out a sigh. "You're lucky," he said. "The cook's assistant has gone home to help with her sister's baby, so we're short in the kitchen. But only for one night, mind!"

Ember nodded earnestly, ignoring the blond girl's disgusted noise. No doubt she'd hoped to see Ember thrown out into the street.

"Perhaps you could lend her a fresh gown, lass," the kind stranger suggested. "Looks like she's in need of one."

The girl spluttered. "I'll do no such thing. It's not my fault if she came trekking out here without provisions, thinking to break the monster's curse in one day." She gave Ember a scornful look. "Thought you'd be married to him by sunset, and rich into the bargain, didn't you?" She sniffed. "I'm glad he gored you with his tusks. Serves you right."

"I didn't come here to help the monster," said Ember, once again irked by the assumption. "And I *certainly* didn't come here to marry him!"

But the angry words petered out as she remembered that nothing was as she'd thought. Haiden hadn't brazenly admitted to being a murderer. He'd admitted to being born with the ability to wield magic, a situation that was neither inherently evil nor within his control. And for that revelation, she'd treated him like...well, like a monster.

"I don't know anything about the rumors of the curse that brought you here," she said more calmly. "I don't have any reason to think that I could help him even if I wanted to, or that doing so would make me rich. And he didn't gore me," she added, honesty compelling her to defend him. "My injuries were inflicted by someone else. In fact, Haiden is the one who treated the wounds."

"Haiden?" The girl stared blankly at her. "Who's that?"

Ember just turned disdainfully away. The other girl hadn't even bothered to find out Haiden's name? Clearly she was only interested in his curse, or whatever benefit she thought she'd gain if she broke it. No wonder Haiden had been in such a bad mood when Ember arrived.

"I don't need a new gown," she said to the barkeep, trying heroically to straighten her ripped and stained skirts. "This one is fine."

He snorted. "Not if you're going to work in my kitchen, it isn't." He put down his rag with a sigh. "You'd best run upstairs, first door on the left. My wife will sort you out. I think our daughter left a few gowns behind when she got married."

"Thank you," said Ember meekly, pausing only to send the kind stranger a tentative smile before following the barkeep's instructions.

## CHAPTER SEVEN

# Ember

Within half an hour, Ember was dressed in a fresh gown of a pleasant blue fabric, and hard at work in the kitchens. Her stomach rumbled as she scrubbed pots under the agitated direction of a stressed cook, but she didn't complain. The barkeep probably wanted her to prove she was going to perform her end of the bargain before feeding her.

By the time she was finally given food, her head was spinning from the hunger. But a hearty stew in the kitchen with the cook helped restore her. The tavern's customers had finished their food and were settling in for an evening of drinking and conversation, so the cook was more relaxed than Ember had seen him all day. Emboldened by his good humor, Ember laid her spoon down.

"Have you lived in this area for long?" she asked casually.

He chortled. "Everyone in Arville has lived here forever," he told her. "We're a small community, and we keep to ourselves."

Reflecting that he had no idea just how much she knew of insular communities, Ember pushed on.

"So has the...the monster been here forever, then?"

The cook shook his head. "That's different. Dunno where he came from, but guess he can't go back there, since he got himself cursed."

"How did he get cursed?" Ember asked.

The cook scratched his chin with the handle of his spoon. "Tried to sail east, to the Reviled Lands, about five years ago. Everyone told him he'd run afoul of the magic protection on those waters, but of course he didn't listen."

Five years ago, like Haiden had said. So who had the Protector and his predecessors been sacrificing maidens to before that? Cold seemed to trickle down Ember's back as she remembered what had happened when she'd been taken to be "sacrificed". Had they all just been murdered and thrown into the ocean?

"What do you mean the magic protection?" she asked. "Why can't people sail east?"

Haiden couldn't be responsible for the protections as the Protector had claimed, given they'd been in place for thirty years, since the Protector had managed to leave and return safely.

The cook shrugged, losing interest. "Don't know why. Most of us aren't foolish enough to test it for ourselves. He did."

"So why do the girls come?" Ember asked. "What do they hope to gain?"

He shrugged again. "Ask the girl upstairs. They want to break his curse, I suppose. Waste of time, if you ask me."

"Why?" Ember pressed.

He sighed, rising from his seat. "He's holed himself up

all alone since the curse, hasn't he? Seems like if he wanted help, he'd ask for it."

Ember frowned, remembering what Haiden had said to her. *I have no intention of helping you with anything, and I most definitely don't want your help.* She'd thought it odd at the time, since she'd given no indication of trying to help him.

"Best get some sleep," the cook told her, as he strolled away from the table. "I'll expect you down here before dawn."

More than exhausted enough to take his advice, Ember made her way to the small room she'd been assigned—once a cupboard, by the looks of it—and surrendered immediately to the sleep tugging at her.

The next morning passed in a blur. Ember was kept busy in the kitchen until past the lunch hour, at which time the barkeep started to give her sideways looks whenever she entered the tavern's main room. Remembering that the arrangement was only for one night, Ember realized she needed to think about her next step, and quickly.

She was glad when the cook sent her to collect an order of fish. Perhaps the walk would help her order her thoughts. She was still determined to help the community she'd left behind on the island, but it was becoming abundantly clear that she couldn't do that alone. In fact, she'd probably struggle to even keep herself alive without help.

And she knew no one on the mainland to whom she could turn for aid.

Her thoughts flew instantly to Haiden. She was foolish to think of him. He'd made it clear he didn't want to help her, even before she'd misguidedly accused him of being a murderer. But he had tended to her injuries while she was unconscious, which was more than the sailors who'd given her passage had done.

The way to the wharf was clear, the sound of the ocean calling her like a familiar friend. Ember got plenty of looks from strangers as she walked, everyone recognizing an outsider. But that wasn't what made her feel unsettled. A sensation grew on her, one she'd felt on the island at times. It was the feeling of being watched, and she became increasingly convinced that someone was following her. But whoever it was remained out of sight every time she looked around.

She reached the wharf at last, eager now to complete her errand and return to the temporary haven of the tavern. She'd just received the fish when a voice hailed her.

"Hey, ocean girl!"

She looked over to see a burly man waving at her. She recognized him as one of the sailors who'd taken her aboard, and returned his wave unenthusiastically.

"Thanks for the boat," he said, grinning. He was making no effort to keep his voice down as he strode toward her, and Ember noticed others watching in interest. "It's a sturdy little craft."

Her answering smile was strained. "I'm glad it's serving you well."

"How are you getting on?" He cast his eyes over her. "You look in better shape than when I last saw you. Did you conquer the monster?"

Ember scowled. "Not exactly."

The man chuckled again. "Cantankerous, isn't he? Comes into town for supplies sometimes, and always in a foul mood."

"Is it true he was cursed trying to sail east through a magic barrier?" Ember asked.

The fisherman nodded. "Oh yes. We all know about the barrier. None of us sail that far east." He squinted up at the sky. "Well, not for decades, anyway. When I was a lad, some fishermen tried it. They were convinced they saw a land mass appear out that way, and decided to discover what it was."

"And?" Ember asked uneasily.

"Never came back," the sailor said. "Lost at sea."

"How...how long ago was this?" Ember asked.

He frowned in an effort of memory. "Well, it was around the time I got my first position on a vessel...maybe thirty years?"

Ember stayed silent, horrified. The men hadn't been lost at sea. They'd reached her island, and been killed by the Protector and his brother. They were the supposed vengeful attacking force from the mainland.

"Anyway, no one's been fool enough to try since," the sailor added comfortably.

"No one but Haiden," said Ember, her voice quiet.

"Who?"

She sighed. "The monster. You said that's how he got cursed."

"Ah, him." The fisherman nodded sagely. "Although in his case, I think there was also an elf involved. Don't remember the details."

"What's an elf?" Ember asked blankly.

The man raised his eyes in disbelief.

"An elf. You know, the little critters who mine magic from the land."

"Magic?" Ember stared at him. "I thought it was singers who could manipulate magic."

The man looked more bemused than ever. "You really don't know what elves are? They don't sing, or manipulate magic directly. They mine it out of the ground, and craft it into talismans to use or sell." He shook his head. "Where did you *come* from on that boat of yours?"

Ember bit her lip, aware that exposing her ignorance made her vulnerable. Before she could think of a reply, the man's gaze slid to something over her shoulder.

"That's an elf," he said, pointing with the spool of netting he was holding.

Ember swirled to see a startling creature listening to their conversation with folded arms. She blinked at him, feeling like she'd wandered into a bedtime story. When the man had called elves *little critters*, she'd pictured some kind of small animal, like a badger or something. The creature before her was much like a human, except perhaps half the size. His skin was very pale, his eyes were vividly green, and his blond hair was streaked with gray. And, Ember noted with amazement, his ears were too long for a human's, tapering into a point at the tip.

"I would also like to know where you came from," the elf said, his voice pitched higher than an adult human's.

Ember didn't answer. Something about him unnerved her, and the thought flitted through her mind that he might have been the one following her.

"What's the matter, got nothing to say?" the elf pressed, his shrewd scrutiny making Ember's skin crawl.

"Careful, lass," muttered the sailor. "You have to take great care what you say to an elf. There's magic about them that can make words binding whether you mean them to be or not."

The way the elf's long ears wobbled convinced Ember that he'd heard the murmured aside. He ignored the sailor, however, his eyes still fixed on Ember.

"He said something about you conquering the monster. Been trying to lift his curse, have you?"

"No." Ember didn't expand on her answer, unsure what was safe to say.

The elf regarded her for a long moment, his expression hard to read.

Uncomfortable, Ember raised her parcel of fish. "I'd best deliver this to the tavern." Bobbing her head in acknowledgment to the sailor, she hurried past the elf.

"Wait."

She'd barely gone out of the fisherman's earshot when she felt a firm grip on her arm. The creature had followed her, his slender hand pulling her to a stop.

"You're from *there*, aren't you?"

The elf's green eyes were narrowed as they studied her face.

"I don't...I don't know where you mean," Ember stammered, her heart hammering. Was it possible the elf knew about the island? Or was he referring to the Reviled Lands? More likely the latter.

The elf considered her for another moment before doing the last thing she expected. Releasing her arm, he squatted down and grabbed at her borrowed gown, his long fingers pinching their way along the seam.

"What are you doing?" she demanded, gathering the fabric and shaking him loose. "Stop that!"

The elf straightened, his eyes shrewd and uncommunicative as he watched her. More unnerved than ever, Ember backed away, turning and breaking into a jog as soon as she was free of him.

She could feel the elf's eyes on her all the way out of the wharf, although he didn't follow her. He'd been uncomfortably interested in her. And not just her—he'd been quick to ask about Haiden as well. Was that the elf who'd had a hand in Haiden's curse? Her thoughts soured further toward the unsettling little stranger.

By the time she reached the tavern, Ember had made a decision. Maybe it was foolish, but her options were limited, and for whatever reason, it was the most appealing course.

She wouldn't wait for the barkeep to kick her out. She would deliver the fish, then go back to the only place on the mainland where she felt no fear of being trapped or exploited, mainly because her presence was so obviously unwelcome.

Haiden's clearing.

# CHAPTER EIGHT

# *Haiden*

Haiden stomped through the undergrowth, taking satisfaction in being unnecessarily destructive. He couldn't remember the last time he'd been in such a bad mood.

And he'd been in a foul temper for the last five years, so that was saying something.

His memory flew to the day before, his mind's eye punishing him with an image of Ember's face when he'd asked if she had a problem with him being a singer.

*How could anyone not?*

Her words had stung enough, but her horrified expression had been worse.

*I don't want or need help from a monster like you.*

Haiden kicked at a bramble as he passed. That was the thanks he got for tending her wounds and letting her sleep in his bed while he shivered in a chair. How dare she look at him like that? How dare she make him feel like a monster?

It was ironic, he reflected. He'd been a monster for years now, and he'd seen similar looks of horror on many faces when he entered their view. But no reaction to his boar-man form had ever upset him as much as Ember's words. Perhaps because in spite of his appearance, it had been the first time Ember had looked at him like he was a monster.

And while he'd never cared much about what he looked like—either before or after the curse—the singing was much more personal.

He'd become begrudgingly accustomed to the series of maidens who'd tried to rescue him over the last five years. But Ember was something else entirely. Who was this maddening nuisance of a girl, who'd sailed into his life full of accusations instead of offers of help, and managed almost immediately to stir up his deepest fears?

For a fleeting moment, the memory of Ember's expression was replaced by an even more painful image...his mother's horrified face the day he'd discovered his song. He'd been only four years old. And he'd seen that same face enough times in the years that had followed to make him wish to forget that time altogether.

So how dare Ember—a singer herself—treat him to the same expression?

His lip curled at her self-delusion, but the humor was short lived. His own turmoil was too all-consuming. He'd thought he was past his old belief that singing made him evil, but it had all resurfaced with Ember's words.

*I don't want or need help from a monster like you.*

She'd said it just as though he'd offered her help, instead of vehemently refusing it when it was demanded, Haiden thought dryly.

Re-entering his clearing, he glanced up instinctively, then berated himself. It was infuriating to realize a part of him was looking for her, as if still hoping she'd come back and tell him she was wrong about him being an abomination.

What did he need her approval for? He didn't. If he never laid eyes on her again, it would be too soon.

Haiden made his way into his cottage, slamming the door so hard the frame rattled. He threw himself down at the small table, grabbing a sheaf of parchment and a stub of lead. He glanced over his many scribbled notes without much enthusiasm. The notes were comprehensive—he didn't think he'd forgotten anything significant of the magic theory he'd learned at the academy back in Teren. But none of it had helped him lift his curse. And he knew he needed to lift his curse before trying again to reach the Reviled Lands if he wanted to avoid being killed on sight.

Assuming he could even get past the magic barrier. He could still remember the crippling pain, although it was hard to know how much of that pain had been from the barrier and how much from the elf's disfiguring curse, given the curse was apparently designed to be triggered by him crossing the barrier. What would happen if he tried to cross it again? Would the curse be further activated? Would he perhaps become a beast in earnest, not just look like one?

His fingers closed reflexively around the stub of lead, and a jolt of horror shot through him as he found himself unable to grip it. His fingers no longer felt familiar, thick hoof-like digits scraping against the tabletop as he quickly withdrew his hand. A moment later, he flexed his fingers to find that normal feeling had returned.

His heart thudded uncomfortably. It was surely just a trick of the mind, caused by the direction of his thoughts. But it was enough to sober him.

The afternoon was well advanced when Haiden stepped out of the cottage again, bent on collecting water from a nearby stream. A flash of red drew his eyes to the tree line, and he stopped dead in his tracks.

"What do you want?" His voice was colored by the rage of realizing his heart had leaped a little at the sight of his visitor.

Ember stepped forward, her hands folded. "I came to apologize," she said.

"I thought you said you'd never trouble me again," Haiden growled.

"Well," Ember reasoned, still assuming an ill-fitting, demure posture, "hopefully my presence won't trouble you this time. Given I've come to apologize."

"It does trouble me," Haiden said curtly. "Now leave."

Ember ignored his words, moving fully into the clearing. "We didn't get off to a very good start. Which was partly my fault," she added quickly, perhaps seeing that he was about to interject. She paused, before adding candidly, "But also partly your fault. For your generally very boorish manners."

She watched him expectantly, the hint of a smile on her freckled face.

"Nothing?" she said, after a prolonged moment of silence. "*Boorish* manners. You know, because you're a..." She gestured at his face. Or rather, a spot a foot above his face. "You look like a boar," she informed him helpfully. "It was funny."

Haiden's face remained expressionless. "Was it?"

Ember sighed. "It seems the curse took your sense of humor as well, which is frankly more tragic than what it did to your face."

"What do you want, Ember?" Haiden growled.

"To apologize," Ember responded promptly. "Like I said."

"You've done that," Haiden pointed out. "And?"

"Well..." Ember gave him a smile that she clearly hoped would be endearing.

Irritatingly, it *was* a little endearing, just like her less-than-subtle attempts at humor. But there was no need for her to know that.

"Well," she tried again, apparently undaunted by his blank reaction, "I wasn't planning to jump right into it. But yes, I do want something. Your help."

"I thought you didn't want or need my help," Haiden said dryly.

"Yes, well, I've changed my mind." That winning smile was back.

Haiden wasn't so easily manipulated. "Forget it." He folded his arms. "Now leave me alone."

"Well, it's difficult for me to do that," Ember explained.

"Why?" Haiden growled.

Ember's reply was once again artless. "Because I have nowhere else to go."

At least she was honest.

"I don't see how that's my problem," Haiden told her ruthlessly.

He could feel himself weakening, some part of him susceptible to her open and cheerful manner. But he wouldn't allow that weakness. He couldn't afford to forget how she'd looked at him when she'd learned who he really was, and all the remembered pain and anger that reaction had stirred up. If he made himself vulnerable to her in any measure, he made himself vulnerable to that same pain again. And he couldn't allow himself to once again entertain mixed feelings over his singing ability, not when his skills were so necessary to his survival.

"Now leave," he said, hardening his voice further.

He strode forward, gripping her shoulder as he'd done once before. She was in a new gown now, of a pale blue color. It had large openings over the shoulders, helpful in identifying which of her shoulders was the uninjured one. As his hand closed on her skin, he noticed irrelevantly that her shoulders were sprinkled with the same freckles that adorned her face.

This thought was soon banished by much more alarming concerns as he realized that his hand once again felt strange and misshapen. The sensation now matched the inhuman hand he could see resting on her bare skin. It was a horrifying contrast. And even more horrifying was Ember's reaction.

"What is that?" she asked, sounding alarmed. She looked down to see Haiden's hairy, hoof-like hand frozen on her shoulder, before her eyes flew to his. "Last time it felt normal. Now it feels..."

She trailed off as Haiden withdrew his hand like it was burned. Anger rose in him again, barely keeping his fear at bay. What was happening to him?

"GET OUT!" he roared. "Leave me alone!"

To his surprise, Ember didn't flee from his enraged shout. She didn't even flinch.

"I understand you don't want me here," she said calmly. "And I don't blame you after how unkindly I spoke to you. But I'm not leaving. I need help, and I truly don't have any other options."

Her measured reaction was more infuriating than yelling would have been. It left Haiden nowhere to go, and made his own continued anger seem foolish and childish. Breathing heavily, he turned from her, striding across the clearing and into his hut without a backward glance. He slammed the door yet again, releasing a quick and quiet song to check that his defenses were in place.

"Haiden."

The muffled voice carried through the closed door. Ember had approached the hut.

"I'm not going anywhere. I'll wait as long as it takes."

"Then you'll be waiting forever!" he called out, aware that he sounded churlish.

"Come on, Haiden." She sounded exasperated now. "Don't you even want to hear me out?"

"No," he snapped.

It occurred to him that she used his name a great deal. It made his heart ache strangely, which only served to irritate him more. He'd heard his name so rarely in the last five years—few of his prospective rescuers bothered to find it out. And he was perfectly aware that in the village, he was simply referred to as the monster.

Ember had fallen quiet, but he knew she was still there. He could just tell. She wouldn't be able to come through his door with the defenses he had in place. Determining to just ignore her, Haiden sat himself at the little table again, folding his arms and tapping one foot. He would wait her out. Eventually she'd lose interest and go.

Everything was silent for another hour—so silent that Haiden wondered if he was mistaken, and Ember had left after all. But just as he was debating opening the door to check, he heard her weary voice.

"It's almost dark, Haiden. And it's starting to get cold. Don't you think you could let me in? Just to talk, if nothing else?"

Haiden hadn't decided on a reply when he felt the unmistakable sensation of magic rushing toward him. He tensed instinctively before his mind reasserted itself, reminding him that the cottage was protected from magical breaches as well as physical ones.

But Ember wasn't inside his hut. Her muffled cry was

followed by a thud, before her voice was cut off in a horrible choking gurgle that had Haiden out of his seat in seconds. Not even thinking it through, he flung open the door and threw himself out.

Ember was still alone, but she was clearly under attack. She was pressed against the wall of his hut, her hands scrabbling at her throat and her eyes wide with fear and confusion. He could see at a glance that she couldn't breathe.

Haiden cast his eyes wildly around the clearing, searching for the source of the magic he could feel coating Ember's form. It had come in a wave from the trees, but he could sense no lingering connection to its source. It had been released to its purpose, and was now acting independently of further instruction.

Another horrible choke from Ember snapped Haiden out of it. Knowing physical proximity would make no difference, he stayed where he was and raised his voice, reaching with his extra sense for the magic he could feel in the ground beneath him. It responded at once, the gesture as natural and familiar as reaching his hand down and picking up dirt with his fist.

The magic flowed up into him, and he sang low and swiftly, crafting it rapidly into a protective enchantment. Out of force of habit, he formed the magic into an invisible bubble around him. He had to focus harder to coax it outward, toward the girl now sliding slowly down the stone wall of his hut.

Color was draining from her face, and Haiden strode forward, his voice frantic as he tried harder to overcome his instinct of self-protection and push the enchantment toward the one who really needed it. As he drew close enough, the bubble expanded with a painful effort.

He felt the moment it connected with the magic still

clawing at Ember. Haiden might have struggled with the exact shape of his enchantment, but there was nothing wrong with the potency. The two bodies of magic collided with an invisible impact that felt violent in Haiden's senses, the attacking one quickly giving way to his shield enchantment. The magic under his control quickly flowed around Ember, encasing her in a bubble of safety.

With great relief, Haiden heard her give a shuddering gasp, drawing in her first proper breath since the magic had appeared. Her eyes were still wide and fearful as she stared up at him, but as her gaze focused, something shifted in her expression. She still looked rattled, even afraid. But the fear wasn't directed at him. She was looking at him with relief, perhaps even with...trust. As if she felt safe now.

It wasn't a reaction he was used to, even before the curse. He couldn't think of the last time anyone had felt safe because of him. He and his sister had grown up in constant fear and uncertainty, and she'd always been the one to try to project confidence, to try to make him feel safe. But he'd always been able to sense the fear that she carried under the surface at all times.

She hadn't been afraid *of* him, and she'd been the fiercest defender of his singing gift. But so often, when her eyes had rested on him, he'd seen her fear. Fear for his safety, fear of what the world would do to him. Fear that she wouldn't be able to protect him.

Of course, he knew now that singers weren't as despised or as universally exploited as they'd been led to believe in their isolated forest upbringing. Once they'd left the forest, he'd stopped trying to hide his ability for fear of the ramifications. But then he'd been cursed. And since that happened, Haiden had become very accustomed to seeing fear in the eyes of everyone who looked at him, albeit for a reason that had nothing to do with his singing.

The way Ember was watching him now—with silent confidence written across her face as she let herself slump weakly against the wall—was something entirely new. Something that had a strange effect on his heart and stirred an instinct buried deep inside him.

"Thank you." Her soft voice was a little raspy after the near-choking. She looked around the empty clearing. "What was that?"

"Magic," Haiden said gruffly, hanging back from her. "A very vile type of magic, crafted for the specific purpose of taking life, I'd say."

Ember shivered, crossing her arms and rubbing her palms over her bare shoulders. Haiden's gaze was drawn to the gesture.

"I suppose some singers are killers after all." There was a wry smile in Ember's voice.

Haiden shook his head. "I don't think that came from a singer. I didn't hear any song."

"Is that...is that what you did?" Ember asked tentatively. "With your voice? Was that a song?"

Haiden nodded silently, feeling self-conscious as she stared up at him in awe.

"It was beautiful."

The whispered compliment was so out of place, it should have made him laugh. But he couldn't find much humor in the situation.

"Mine was the only song in play, I'm fairly certain," he said. "Judging by the sudden and absolute release of that magic, I think it was a talisman." He frowned. "Which means it could have been wielded by anyone."

"It was definitely magic, though?" Ember asked.

He nodded. "Undoubtedly. I felt it before it hit you. Even from inside my house."

She shivered again. "I felt it, too, although I didn't know what I was feeling. It was like something rushing toward me, something that felt a lot like the sensation that came over me on the ocean." She swallowed. "Until it hit me, and then it felt very different."

Haiden frowned at her. "On the ocean? What do you mean?"

She looked up at him, her expression still relaxed and trusting. It made him feel restless, seeing her so calm. She was so alone and vulnerable, slumped against the wall, still weakened from the vicious attack against which she'd had no defense without his intervention.

"When I was sailing here from my island, there was a moment when I felt something invisible wash over me. I thought it was rain pouring suddenly down, but there was no rain. And it passed quickly. I thought maybe I'd imagined it. I wasn't in the best state."

Haiden felt his frown grow. "You were very injured when you arrived here. What had happened to your leg? It looked like a knife wound."

She bit her lip, yet another shudder passing over her as she saw something in her mind's eye that he couldn't. "It was a knife wound."

"Who did that to you?" Haiden could hear how inhuman the growl sounded, but he didn't care. "Was it the fishermen you mentioned?" In his mind, he ran through all the fishermen he'd seen in Arville, wondering which one was in need of a visit from the monster.

Ember shook her head. "No," she said softly. "It was before that. And it's a long story. Long enough to cover my whole life, and my parents' before mine, really. I'm not ready to get into it." She closed her eyes and laid her head back against the wall. "Not tonight."

Haiden took advantage of the moment to study her face unobserved. It was drawn and pale enough to make her freckles stand out more strongly, even in the moonlight. Her hair was a chaos of curls around her face, but she didn't look like she'd taken any lasting hurt from the attack.

That was a huge relief, for some reason.

"But you said you felt the magic of the barrier, out on the ocean?" he asked, feeling a foolish need for her to open her eyes and speak to him again, to give him some sign of life beyond the steady rise and fall of her chest.

"Yes." She lifted her head, her eyes opening at last. "If that's what it was." Her gaze was tentative as it settled on the spot above his head. "Was that...was that because I'm a singer?"

"Yes," said Haiden shortly. He glanced from her to his open door, drawing in a breath. Even if she was telling the truth that she hadn't come all the way from the Reviled Lands, there was no doubt she knew things he didn't about the seas to the east. Things that he should know before he tried again to sail away from Providore.

There was also no doubt that she wasn't safe out here alone.

"There's a great deal for us to discuss," he said gruffly. He extended a hand.

Ember stared at it for a long moment before reaching out her own. Haiden winced slightly as their hands made contact, but his fingers felt firm and familiar as they closed around her cold ones, and she had no startled reaction this time. His muscles tensing, he pulled her to her feet.

"I have food," he said, the words rough and his tone far from generous as he dropped her hand and strode into the hut. He directed his next words over his shoulder. "You can stay, but for one night only."

His eyes were already looking forward again, but he could almost feel her answering smile.

"Yes, Monster," she said meekly, as she followed him over the threshold.

## CHAPTER NINE

# Ember

Ember's smile faded as she stepped into Haiden's hut. She no longer felt afraid, knowing the dwelling to be magically protected. The source of her discomfort was more along the lines of...awkwardness. Being invited inside and coming willingly was somehow a very different experience from being carried unconscious over the threshold.

Neither she nor Haiden spoke as he laid a simple meal of bread and cheese onto two plates. His grotesque and oversized form was almost comical in the little kitchen. As they ate, Ember glanced around the room. It was as she remembered from her previous visit—simple, and sparsely furnished. There were two main areas to the dwelling, no door between them. She could see a table and chair in the next room, and the space where she currently stood, just inside the door to outside, seemed to serve as both kitchen and bedroom. There was a small fireplace, with a blackened pot hung over it, and a few mounted cupboards with a counter underneath them. Not far from the fireplace was the small bed, no bigger than the one she'd slept in back home.

There was certainly no spare bed.

"Do you...um...have a settee or anything?" Ember asked, leaning sideways for a better look into the next room.

"No." Haiden's reply was curt. "You'll have to sleep in my bed."

Heat rushed over Ember at the matter-of-fact words, and she found herself unable to meet his eye.

"I don't think that's the best idea." She bit her lip, deciding it was best to be frank. "I, uh, I met one of the girls you mentioned, in the tavern in town."

Haiden let out a groan. "The blond one? She's still hanging around?"

Ember nodded, still not looking at his boar-face. "Anyway, I know what those other girls come for, but I didn't come for...that purpose. I don't want to become your bride for some kind of fabulous reward." She added quickly, "No offense."

"None taken," Haiden said dryly. "And you're more sensible than they are, because I'm not some kind of hidden prince, and I have no reason to think any fabulous reward would be involved in breaking my curse." He paused, adding reflectively, "Or marrying me."

The uncomfortable silence stretched on for another moment before he put Ember out of her misery.

"What I meant was that you could use the bed tonight while I sleep on blankets in the other room," he said, a touch of humor in his voice. "Even I'm not such a monster as to expect you to share a bed with a monster."

"I didn't...that's not what I..." Ember stammered.

"Isn't it? No need to be coy."

Haiden's cool haughtiness ignited Ember's own defiance.

"No need to be coy, is there? If you'd prefer me to speak plainly, the idea of sharing the bed was ludicrous from the start, since I can't comprehend how you can fit your monstrous bulk in that bed even without anyone else in the equation."

Haiden let out a snort that almost sounded like stifled laughter. "Not everything is as it appears," he said, already turning toward the other room.

Ember hovered in place for a minute as she listened to him making preparations. She was tempted to peek in and see if he really did have blankets to sleep on, but thought she'd better refrain. When everything went still in the other room, she moved to the bed, sitting tentatively on the edge.

"Politeness probably dictates that I should offer to sleep on the blankets rather than take your bed, doesn't it?" she said into the silence.

"Probably."

Ember scowled at the gruff reply. He wasn't going to give anything for free, was he? She pushed back the ungenerous thought, reminding herself that he was in fact giving up his bed for her. He just wasn't going to pander to her guilt in the process, and she couldn't really blame him for that. In fact, she found she respected him more for it. Back on the island, politeness was paramount, everyone always so focused on how things appeared. Only now she'd left was she fully grasping just how deceitful things were under that respectable surface.

She'd prefer Haiden's impolite honesty over island life any day. Not least because she could probably get away with the same approach when in his company.

"I don't think I will offer, though," she said frankly. "I

can handle being impolite better than I can handle sleeping on the floor."

A grunt was the only reply, once again carrying the hint of a laugh. Ember kicked off her boots, weariness creeping over her now the prospect of sleep was so near. She hadn't been lying down for long when the sound of movement made her lean up on one arm.

"Don't be alarmed." Haiden's voice was still gruff, his misshapen form appearing in the doorway between the rooms. "I'm just going to check the clearing before I retire."

Ember nodded, sitting up and pulling the covers around her for warmth. She watched as Haiden disappeared into the clearing, not even trying to lie down. Her mind was far from rest, and it had nothing to do with guilt over the sleeping arrangements. She kept going over the attack outside the cottage, and Haiden's intervention. She could feel her legs shaking, her body responding belatedly to the realization that she'd almost died that evening.

It was only a few minutes before the door swung open again, and Ember felt herself relax when she saw Haiden's figure silhouetted by the moonlight. He shut the door behind him with a snap.

"There's no one nearby," he said. "I'll retire now." He moved across the room, toward his makeshift sleeping quarters.

"Wait."

Ember's hand shot out as he passed, closing over his arm. She felt him stiffen under the touch, and for a moment she was too distracted to continue what she'd been going to say. She kept her hold on his arm, her thumb moving slowly over the surface in fascinated confusion.

Her touch completely belied the evidence of her eyes. He still wore a short-sleeved tunic from the warm day, and she'd grabbed him down near his wrist. His arm should have been hairy and coarse, not to mention thick as a small tree branch. But what she felt was human skin, warm from his patrol around the clearing, and covered only with the thin layer of hair one would expect on a grown man. Her fingers didn't reach all the way around his arm, but she could tell it wasn't nearly as thick as what her eyes suggested.

His muscles were tensing noticeably, and she released him, leaning back. Questions as to his cursed condition burned in her mind, but she forced herself to instead say what she'd decided had to be said before she could sleep.

"I apologized earlier for the unkind things I said about you being a singer," she said in a rush. "But I don't feel I did it properly."

"It's fine." Haiden's impatience was clear in his reply, but she didn't let that deter her.

"No, it isn't. Because my apology means nothing without an explanation."

She looked earnestly up at him, ignoring his boar-man face and focusing on his very human eyes. Their expression wasn't encouraging, but she pushed on.

"I reacted that way because I thought you were a killer."

"I'm not a killer," Haiden said abruptly. The offense in his voice was rendered a little comical when he added, "Not thus far, at least."

"I believe you," said Ember seriously. "But I misunderstood last time. On the island where I grew up, we know nothing about the world outside except what the leaders tell us. We've heard of singers, although there aren't any in our community. All my life, I was taught that singing is an aberration some people are born with, that gives them the capacity to kill another human. That no one else is capable of that, and that it's deep in the nature of a singer to kill." She tried to infuse her voice with the contrition she felt. "I thought you were telling me, without shame, that you were a murderer by nature, that you'd even studied to hone your craft. Now I know how far from true that is, I also know how cruel my words were. It truly was a misunderstanding on my part."

There was a long moment of silence, but at least now Haiden was looking directly at her.

"Is that honestly what you thought singing meant?" he asked at last.

She nodded. "I only learned the true meaning after I stormed out of here. They told me in the tavern." She shook her head in disbelief. "I had no idea there was any connection between singing and magic."

Haiden's unnatural lips pulled tight in a frown. "What a strange lie for the leaders to tell your community."

"Yes," Ember agreed. "It was used to explain where we came from. Apparently the land our ancestors came from was ravaged by a rebellion, where singers rose up against the rulers and took over, destroying everything in their path. But I suspect now that it's all a lie."

"No." To her surprise, Haiden shook his head. "That part is true. I mean, I don't know how ravaged the land was, or the details of the rebellion. But the reason the Reviled Lands were cut off from this continent is that the singers forcefully overthrew the rulers and took control. The various monarchs here don't want any of Providore's singers getting any ideas." He shrugged. "But although the singers obviously used magic to bring about their coup, that has nothing to do with any innate capacity or preference for killing."

Ember didn't reply, her gaze now on her lap even

though she could feel his eyes boring into her. When he spoke again, his voice was gentler, although it had lost none of its gruff quality.

"I regret to be the one to tell you this, but every human being has the capacity to kill."

"Yes," she whispered, remembering how the Protector's brother had turned on her. "I'm beginning to comprehend that."

"Most choose never to do it," Haiden pointed out. "Which surely means more than not harming others simply because you weren't born with the capacity to do it."

"Yes." Ember raised her eyes to his, feeling heartened. "I suppose that's true." She studied his face in the moonlight slanting through the hut's one small window.

"I'm glad you explained," Haiden said abruptly. "I don't hold it against you that you were taught lies. I also grew up without much exposure to the world."

Ember nodded. "Thank you." She was desperately curious about his childhood, but she'd paid enough attention to realize it wasn't a good idea to press for details.

"There's a reason I've taken a particular interest in the history of the Reviled Lands," Haiden went on, sounding uncomfortable with his own decision to share the information. "My mother's family were descended from there. They fled to the mainland when the coup happened. She was never taught any nonsense about singing and murder being the same thing, but much like you, she was raised to believe that singers were the enemy who'd destroyed everything."

He didn't say more, but he didn't need to. Ember grasped at once how devastated Haiden's mother must have been to have a son who was a singer. And with her own experience of disappointing her parents at every turn, it didn't take much imagination to see how that might affect

Haiden. Something twisted uncomfortably in her heart at the thought of the child Haiden growing up with a mother who hated—and probably feared—his magical gift.

"I see," she said softly. She tried to smile. "It seems we come from common stock, a long way back. Everyone on my island is descended from those who fled the Reviled Lands. We just never made it as far as Providore." She shook her head slowly. "It seems the tale we were told—that our ancestry would make us hated, even hunted, on the mainland—was another lie."

Haiden shrugged. "There was a great deal of suspicion when our ancestors first made it here. My mother was raised to think her ancestry, while a source of private pride, shouldn't be advertised. But when I made it out of our isolated home, I soon learned that her fears were wildly exaggerated. Perhaps some prejudice lingers here and there, but mostly no one cares. It's so many generations ago, we've well and truly intermingled with the rest of the inhabitants of Providore."

Ember nodded, not speaking her thoughts. However uncommon the prejudice against singers and their magic might be, thanks to his mother, it had undoubtedly defined Haiden's whole world. Just as the island's lies had defined hers.

Her eyes were unfocused as they stared out the window. It was hard to take it all in.

"Anyway, you should sleep," Haiden said. "Your body will need as much rest as it can get to recover from that attack." He hesitated for a moment, his voice becoming even gruffer. "You can sleep without fear. You'll be safe in my home."

Ember brought her gaze to his face, her eyes coming into focus again. She'd been going to thank him, but the words died on her lips. She could only stare in shock as the boar-like face wavered before her eyes. Another visage appeared momentarily in the moonlight, noticeably lower than the ghastly face had been. She caught a glimpse of dark skin, heavy brows, and defined cheekbones before the image flickered back to the animal features she knew.

"I..." Ember blinked rapidly, wondering if she'd imagined it. Both mind and emotions certainly felt stretched to their limit. "Thank you," she finished lamely.

With a curt nod, Haiden—fully restored to all seven feet of his boar-like features—strode from the room.

Ember fell back into the bed at last, her mind swirling and her heart beating a little too quickly. Between the memory of that serious face, and the phantom feel of Haiden's arm under her fingers, it took her some time to settle enough for sleep. It was impossible not to be kept awake by the many mysteries and contradictions surrounding her host. As she finally began to drift, her last thought was that the bed had a subtle scent about it, one that was somehow already becoming both familiar and comforting.

And it wasn't any smell she would associate with a pig, or any other animal Gil might raise on his farm back on the island. It was decidedly human, and decidedly Haiden.

# CHAPTER TEN

# Ember

Ember woke slowly, her mind struggling to emerge from sleep. She blinked slowly in the dim light, trying to recapture the vivid images of her dreams. They'd been haunted by a face, one she'd seen only the briefest catch of, but which was burned in her memory nonetheless.

The rough walls of Haiden's hut came into view. Judging by the low light, dawn was only just breaking. She sat up, listening, but she heard no sound of movement from the other room. The need to relieve herself precluded any possibility of returning to sleep, and she slipped on her boots. She didn't make straight for the door, however. Instead, she found herself creeping toward the hut's second area.

Haiden lay sprawled across the floor, fast asleep. His monstrous form took up most of the small room. Ember hovered in the doorway, studying his boar-like features with intense focus, willing the image to flicker and display a human face again.

Nothing.

Sighing at her own foolishness, Ember backed up, slipping out the door and into the clearing. The trees surrounding the hut ensured that no hint of the sun could yet reach her, but she could see signs of it in the sky. The day would begin soon. And what it would bring, Ember couldn't guess. She hurried through the trees, chafing her hands against the cold as she looked for a private enough place for her needs.

On the way back, she paused to collect a fallen branch from the undergrowth. She'd noted before leaving the hut that the fire had all but burned out. They'd need to stoke it if they planned to cook breakfast, which Ember was very much hoping they were.

She'd gathered a decent armful of sticks by the time she emerged back into the clearing. Her mind was on her host, wondering if he'd woken yet, and she was taken completely by surprise when a shape burst from the trees nearby. Ember hardly had time to take in a second figure following the first before they were upon her.

One of the men grabbed her, his strong arm circling her waist and yanking her back against him. Ember dropped the wood, retaining her hold on one stick, which she flailed wildly around her. But the second man approached, ripping it from her hand. He was enormous, with thick arms and broad shoulders, and she saw at once that she'd never be able to fight him off. She'd never been trained to defend herself, and she had no weapon.

She was just sucking in her breath when the man holding her slapped a hand over her mouth, silencing her with embarrassing ease.

"Do it, quick," he grunted.

To Ember's horror, a third man came into her vision, this one of a more wily build, but no less intimidating.

Perhaps because of the blade he held, pointed purposefully in Ember's direction.

Forcing back her panic, Ember thrashed wildly, kicking her legs back against the shins of her captor. He grunted as she connected, but his hold didn't waver. She couldn't outmatch only him, let alone all three. She needed help.

Help.

Haiden!

Ember switched her focus from her limbs to her head, wrenching it around violently. The change was unexpected enough that she managed to loosen the hold on her mouth slightly—an opportunity she didn't waste as she bit down hard on his hand.

The stranger let out a cry, his hand yanking away instinctively. Ignoring the vile taste in her mouth, and the puncture wounds her teeth had made on his palm, Ember raised her voice in the loudest scream she could muster.

"HELP!"

Cursing, the man slapped his hand back over her mouth. The one with the blade swore as well, but instead of plunging the knife straight into Ember, he glanced at the hut, obviously concerned he might need to defend his back.

That moment's hesitation was enough. With a bang that sent birds fluttering from the trees, the door to the hut flew violently open. Ember's heart swelled with relief as Haiden's hideous form launched from the dwelling.

He took in the scene at a glance, letting out a roar inhuman enough to justify the title of monster. In a few swift strides, he crossed the clearing, his voice shifting into a song that was no less angry. It was the most intense sound she'd ever heard, nothing like his song the night before. She'd thought that one beautiful and mesmerizing, but this one put it to shame. Something fierce and wild rose up in her in response. She could feel her own song, trapped, clamoring to be free, like a much more intense version of the impulse that had caused her to mimic the bird that fateful day on the island.

For the first time, she fully believed it.

She was a singer.

She was a singer, and it was nothing to be ashamed or afraid of. Unless you were an attacking enemy, of course, like the man who was currently face down in the dirt, his blade useless beside him as an invisible force pressed him into the ground.

Ember curbed the impulse to sing, afraid to interfere with whatever Haiden was doing. He certainly seemed to be managing fine on his own. His magical attack on the man with the blade hadn't slowed his physical advance at all. The second man turned to face him, but his raised fists proved useless against Haiden's fury. With a single swipe, he sent the man flying into a tree with a sickening thud.

Ember let out a gasp as she felt the tip of a blade touch her neck. She hadn't even realized that the man holding her had a weapon of his own. Apparently he wasn't going to give up without a fight.

"Stop there, or she dies," he growled at the advancing monster.

Haiden, with a cool that deeply impressed Ember, didn't grace this threat with a response. He'd just reached the first man, and he stopped to kick his blade out of reach before placing one hoofed foot on his neck. All the while his song continued, low and throbbing.

"I said *stop!*" the man holding Ember cried, his grip around her waist tightening.

Haiden looked up, meeting his eyes at last. He brought his song to a graceful conclusion, his foot remaining on the downed man. He gave every appearance of calm, but Ember wasn't fooled. She could see the fury in his eyes, and it sent a strange thrill through her. She'd thought he was angry with her when she intruded on his peace, but she saw now that what he'd felt toward her had been nothing more than petty annoyance. It paled in comparison to the anger he felt *for* her.

"Now back away, or she gets it," the stranger demanded, apparently believing himself to have the upper hand.

Haiden's eyes strayed to the dagger against Ember's throat, his focus intense. It took Ember a moment to realize that the low hum she heard was coming from him. He was barely moving his lips. Her captor suddenly realized it, too, but his warning growl turned quickly into a shout of fear.

Ember could understand why. Horror washed over her as she heard a hissing near her ear. The man loosened his grip enough for her to pull away, and she yanked herself free, staring at the snake now curled around the stranger's hand. There was no sign of the blade.

The man dropped the snake, shaking his hand in his frantic efforts to fully dislodge it. He was completely focused on the serpent writhing in the grass, and the next thing Ember knew, Haiden's hoof-like fist was curled around the man's throat. His grip elicited a sputtering gurgle that she could barely hear over the growl of rage that had replaced Haiden's song. The stranger's face was losing color rapidly, and Ember found herself stumbling forward.

"Stop!" she urged. She grabbed Haiden's arm, once again noting the human feel of it. "He can't breathe."

"I know," growled Haiden. "That's the idea."

"Stop," she said again, the word a command this time.

"Why should I?" he demanded. "Don't you realize they were trying to kill you?"

"Of course I realize," Ember said impatiently. "It's not them I'm thinking of. It's you. You told me that you're not a killer, and I believe you."

Something in her words seemed to get through, and he finally loosened his grip. For the briefest moment, Ember thought his face flickered again, the one from her dreams appearing for a solitary heartbeat. Then her former attacker drew in a shuddering breath, and her attention returned to him, on his knees and clutching at his bruised throat. Ember followed his gaze and was astonished to see the dagger lying motionless where the snake had been.

"Was it ever a snake?" she asked, amazed. "Or just an illusion?"

"Illusion magic is much more powerful than people realize," Haiden said, the words clipped. He didn't look at her, his narrowed eyes fixed on the stranger. "Who hired you?"

The man shook his head, his hands still cradling his neck. "I don't know," he croaked. "We never saw them. Written instructions with a pouch of gold. Half before, half..." his eyes flicked to Ember, "after."

She folded her arms, glaring. "After what? After you murdered me?"

The man didn't reply, his demeanor fearful and his eyes riveted on Haiden. Looking behind her, Ember saw that the man who'd been knocked out against the tree was stirring, and the one who'd been pressed into the dirt was picking himself up.

"Get out," Haiden growled. "All of you. If I see your faces again, you die." They'd already started edging away, but he added for good measure, "And I'm placing a curse on you. Next time you try to harm someone for money, your own blades will turn against you and kill you."

The words morphed seamlessly into a song, the words somewhat gruesome and the tune low and angry. The men didn't need to be told twice. They sprinted into the trees in disorder.

Haiden's song petered out as soon as they were gone, and he turned toward Ember.

"Are you all right?" he asked gruffly, taking hold of her shoulders and searching her face.

She nodded, running her hands gingerly over her waist where the man had gripped her.

"Are you sure?" he pressed. "Did they hurt you?"

"I'm sure." She was pleased that her voice came out confident. "I'm not hurt. Just...rattled." She gave him a rueful smile. "You probably don't believe me, but my life has actually been very uninteresting up until recently. A week ago, no one had ever tried to kill me. Now it's happened three times."

Haiden's lips pulled back to reveal his fang-like teeth, the expression apparently a grimace.

"We need to prioritize you learning your craft. You can't keep walking around defenseless."

Ember sighed. She should probably be offended at this description of her, but it was too apt for her to protest.

"Did you really place a curse on them?" she asked. "Will it really stop them from killing?"

Haiden snorted. "Of course not. I don't think a curse like that even exists. But they won't know that. It might make them pause."

Ember stared into the trees, disconcerted. "Or it might not. Maybe we should report them in town."

"Do whatever you like," said Haiden dismissively. "But they were certainly not from Arville. Passing bandits, most likely. And they won't stick around for whoever hired them to discover they took half the payment and didn't finish the job. I doubt there's anything anyone in town can do."

"We shouldn't have let them go," said Ember anxiously. "What if they kill someone else?"

"You're the one who wouldn't let me kill them," Haiden pointed out, indignant. "You can't complain now that I let them go. What did you think I'd do, build a prison in the clearing?"

She sighed. "I suppose not. But someone had to curb your temper." Her gaze became shrewd as she studied his boar-like face. The sun had risen in earnest now, and the clearing was bathed in a muted light. Not that it made his inhuman features any easier to read. "Why did you care so much, anyway? You must have realized they weren't after you, but me."

Haiden gave a gruff grunt, stepping back from her. "It's a matter of principle. I said you would be safe in my home." His eyes grew stormy, and his voice was suddenly tinged with anger. "Speaking of which, what were you thinking, going outside alone? After last night, you should have known something like this would happen! How could you be so foolish as to leave the hut?"

Ember folded her hands, her expression meek. "I'm very sorry for being so silly, and causing you such inconvenience," she said.

He narrowed his eyes, clearly suspicious of her submissive response. As well he should be.

"It's no use talking to you," he said impatiently. "You'd better get back inside before someone else tries to kill you. I have some eggs we can cook for breakfast."

"All right," Ember said, not quite succeeding in hiding her smile.

She gave up the attempt altogether when Haiden turned

away from her, allowing herself to grin at his back as she followed him. She wasn't deceived by the return of his brusqueness or his apparent anger. Having seen what made him truly angry, she had no fear that any quirk or misstep of hers would genuinely trigger his rage.

And in spite of the ordeal she'd just been through, she didn't feel afraid. Instead, she felt warmed to know that in a moment of need, Haiden hadn't hesitated to charge to her aid. For someone who'd claimed to be set against helping her, he'd been very quick to respond to her scream.

Half an hour later, she found herself seated at the small table in Haiden's hut, looking at her host over a plate of food.

"I think it's time you tell me how you ended up here," Haiden said curtly. "The plain and simple truth, please."

Ember nodded her agreement. "I owe you that much."

Between mouthfuls, she told him about life on the island, their history, the sacrifice tradition, and the ceremony during which she was chosen. She told him what had happened when the Protector's brother rowed her out onto the ocean, and how she'd escaped. He listened silently, only the odd grunt or grimace giving any indication of his reaction.

"The talk of a monster protecting the island is almost certainly nonsense," he said, when she was at last done. "And it definitely has nothing to do with me. Like I told you, I've only been in this state for five years."

Ember rubbed her face, pushing away her long-since empty plate. "Well, something's been shielding the island. No one's gotten through since that unfortunate boatload of men thirty years ago."

Haiden nodded. "I've heard that tale. It confirmed the local belief that to sail east means certain death."

"It did for them," Ember said sadly.

Haiden ignored this. "That leader of yours did something when he came here, no doubt. But it wasn't a deal with a monster."

"He couldn't have created the barrier from the mainland," Ember said. "The only magic he has comes from the island itself, and only when it's needed for community decisions, like the ceremony where sacrifices are chosen."

Haiden let out a scoff. "That's not some deep magic from the land. What you described sounds like a simple indicating talisman."

"A what?" Ember asked, bewildered.

"A talisman to identify something," Haiden said. "It's a glorified way for the wielder to point at something. The instructors at the academy I attended used them all the time, to point to the student they wanted to answer a question, or to identify something across the room when teaching. Very simple magic, not even expensive to buy. Your Protector probably picked some up when he came to the mainland. These selection ceremonies were just a paltry trick. Someone out of sight would have been wielding the talisman, and pointed it at the person they wanted chosen."

Ember froze, mortification washing over her. Was that why the Protector's brother had been absent from the ceremony? So he could use some cheap talisman to point at her? She knew Haiden hadn't caused the situation he was explaining, but anger still bubbled within her. It was galling to hear him speak so scornfully of the cataclysmic event that had changed her life forever.

"A paltry trick?" she repeated, her voice impassioned. "Then it's a paltry trick with which he's controlled an entire community for decades! People's lives have been in his hands, and some have died from his schemes. The magic may be paltry to someone as educated as you, but it wasn't paltry in impact."

There was a moment of silence as Haiden processed her change in mood. She kept her eyes on her plate, half of her ashamed of her outburst, the other half still angry.

"I'm sorry."

The unexpected apology brought Ember's head whipping up. It was the most surprising thing Haiden had done since she met him.

"I spoke thoughtlessly. I know it's not a trivial matter for you," he went on. He glanced eastward, toward the distant and invisible coast. "Someone else also doesn't consider it trivial, given you've been attacked twice since your visit to Arville." He returned his gaze to her, frowning. "Someone didn't want you to tell me—or anyone—all of this."

Ember considered it. "You think whoever tried to kill me did it to keep my island secret? But that means someone knows about my island. I thought everyone who did was there, not here."

"Did you tell anyone in Arville?" Haiden asked.

She shook her head. "I was careful not to. But I did see one of the fishermen who found me on the water and brought me to shore. He knows I came from somewhere in my boat, although he doesn't know where." Unease shot over her as she remembered the conversation at the wharf. "And the elf seemed to have his suspicions about where I'd come from, too. I assumed he thought I was from the Reviled Lands, but maybe—"

"What elf?" Haiden interrupted sharply.

She let out a long breath. "There was an elf at the wharf. I think he followed me from the tavern. He asked about where I came from." Her eyes flicked to his. "And about you."

"So he's showed his face again, has he?" Haiden's voice was stormy, but after a moment, his eyes became more contemplative than angry. "What's brought him into the open, I wonder? Is it your arrival?"

"You think he's the one who had a hand in your curse?" Ember asked quickly.

Haiden's eyes shot to her, but he didn't comment on her newfound knowledge about his curse. "Undoubtedly. Arville doesn't get a lot of elves. When I first came here, I had the impression he'd been based in the area for a long time, and I have reason to think he's still nearby, keeping an eye on everything." He brought his hand down on the table in a decisive gesture. "He's probably the one trying to get rid of you."

"But why?" Ember demanded, aghast. "What does he have against me? How could he even know about the island? I'm sure he's never been there."

"We can figure out the why later," Haiden said. "The first priority, like I said, is for you to learn to defend yourself. You need to learn some songcraft."

"Does that mean you're going to help me free my island?" Ember asked hopefully.

He gave a noncommittal grunt. "No, it just means I'm going to let you stay here until I get to the bottom of what that elf is mixed up in."

"I'll take it," said Ember briskly. "When do we start training?"

Haiden stood. "Now."

# CHAPTER ELEVEN

# Ember

Excited, Ember followed Haiden out into what was proving to be a sunny morning.

"The magic comes from the ground," Haiden said, as soon as they were outside. He squatted down with his palms against the dirt, the sight comical given his hulking shape. "Try to feel it."

Ember copied his gesture, hiking up her skirts to better get down to ground level. She pushed her fingers into the dirt, closing her eyes.

"I don't really know what I'm supposed to be trying to feel," she said, after a prolonged moment of silence. She looked up to find Haiden rocking back on his heels.

"Hm. It's difficult to know where to start, given you've quite possibly had no exposure whatsoever. You say there are no other singers on your island?"

"That's right," Ember said.

Haiden seemed skeptical. "And yet, it's in your blood, so it came from somewhere. It can skip generations, sometimes several. But it's definitely in the bloodline at some point. And I'd be surprised if you're the only one."

"Wouldn't I know if there were others?" Ember demanded.

He shrugged. "Not necessarily. They might not even know. You didn't, right? It may have gone unnoticed for their whole lives if it was never activated. Usually children discover their singing gift when they hear someone else sing, or hear music, and try to sing along without knowing why. That's how it happened for me."

"And for me, I suppose," said Ember, struck. "But in my case it was a bird."

"I've never heard of a bird triggering it for anyone before," said Haiden. "Or of it being undiscovered until your age. Which suggests that opportunities for it to be identified in the normal ways were nonexistent."

He narrowed his eyes in thought. "I wonder if there *was* magic in the ground on your island. I've never heard of any land completely devoid of it. But there must be some if you managed to mimic the bird at all."

He sighed, gesturing with his ghastly head. "Try again."

Obediently, Ember pressed her hands into the dirt and closed her eyes again. They flickered back open in surprise a moment later when a low, melodic song issued from her companion.

It was beautiful. Haunting and soulful. It felt like an embodiment of the land itself. As she focused on it, she could almost feel the essence of the ground beneath them rising up and into Haiden. Not into, she realized, but through. His voice released into the world.

"I feel it!" she said, excited. "Not for myself, but I can sort of...sense...the magic passing from the ground into you, then out."

Haiden nodded, his song dying out. "Good. That proves that you have the susceptibility to magic. Only singers can sense its presence like that. Now we just have to work on you learning to sense it for yourself. It will take a while for your mind to comprehend that it's accessible to you. Maybe we would do better to focus first on your actual singing."

"All right," said Ember.

"So let's hear it," Haiden prompted, when the silence stretched out. "Sing."

"Uh..." Ember rubbed the back of her neck, self-conscious. "I don't really know how."

He frowned. "I don't really know how to teach you. Like I've said, I've never come across someone who's reached adulthood before discovering their singing ability." He considered her. "The best way I can think to describe it is that there's a song inside you, and it wants to be released. Try to find it, and just let it out."

"That's your best explanation?" Ember said, exasperated.

Haiden just shrugged.

With a sigh, Ember turned her focus inward. Embarrassed by his scrutiny, she closed her eyes. She loved how it sounded when Haiden sang. It was so much more rhythmic and mesmerizing than speaking. Like speech that had learned to dance. When she'd been under attack that morning, and Haiden had come to her aid, she'd felt the urge to join in. But now, in the calm quiet of the clearing, with no threat and no strong emotion, it was hard to conjure up that impulse.

"Don't think about it." Haiden's voice was soft, and closer to her than she expected. Resolutely, she kept her eyes closed, which took all her willpower when she felt his hand splay over hers where it rested on the dirt. "Just sing."

Somehow, with his voice so low and close, and his hand warm and smooth over hers, his monstrous countenance ceased to exist. It wasn't just that she couldn't see it with her eyes closed. She didn't believe—couldn't believe—that a cursed man with a boar's head was inches from her. It was a human, strong and steady and familiar.

The face she'd seen a glimpse of the night before flashed before her eyes, and hard on its heels was a burst of emotion as she remembered what she'd felt when he'd appeared in the doorway that morning.

Ember didn't try to sort through her feelings. Instead she poured them into her voice. Opening her mouth, she let out a call, imagining herself winging into the sky along with her voice, as free as the birds she'd once mimicked.

The sound that came out was strange, but familiar. Like catching at a dream that was slipping away. She knew she'd never made a sound like it, but she could have sworn she'd heard it before.

And, even more exciting than what her voice was doing, was the stirring she felt beneath her. A little rush of energy passed up from the ground and into her body, before flying upward and out of her reach. It was like a reverse version of the sensation she'd once thought was rain falling on her and her boat.

"Did I do it?" she asked, her eyes still squeezed tightly. "Did I sing?"

"You did." Haiden's voice, still very close by, sounded amused. "It was a little off-key, but it was definitely singing."

"What's off-key?" Ember asked.

He gave a low chuckle. "Never mind. It's something they teach at the academy."

"I want to try again," Ember said eagerly.

"Good." She could hear the approval in his voice. "Go ahead."

Ember squeezed her eyes even more tightly shut, once again leaning into her emotion as she raised her voice.

This time the rush of power from the ground was immediate. It didn't feel like a huge amount—nothing like the torrent that had raced toward her and tried to strangle her the night before. But it was undeniably responding to her call, passing into her and out.

Her eyes flew open, her voice still issuing from her throat as she excitedly sought Haiden's reaction.

Her pride over her achievement trickled away. Haiden's voice had told her he was near, but that hadn't prepared her for the face that would meet her eyes. Not only was it close to hers, it was nothing like the boar features she'd become used to. It was the face she'd seen in glimpses, but now it was fully visible. She stared, taking in the dark, soulful eyes, the strong brows, the determined chin framed by scruffy black hair. His skin was much darker than her own freckled visage, and his ruffled hair had a thickness that made her want to run her fingers through it. As she drank in every detail, his brows drew together in confusion, the eyes—the only unchanged part of him—meeting hers uncertainly.

Ember was hardly even aware of the fact that she was still singing, her voice coming out in a wordless hum as she slowly lifted the hand not trapped under Haiden's. She reached out, her fingertips brushing the smooth skin of his cheek, just above the scruffy beard.

At once Haiden reared back, yanking his hand from hers and hastening to his feet.

"What are you doing?" he demanded.

Ember's song petered out, and before her eyes, Haiden's face disappeared. The boar's features that replaced it sat well above where his head had been a moment before, the rest of his form unnaturally enlarged as well.

"I...I saw you," she stammered, her heart racing both from what she'd seen and from the anger still in his eyes. "Your real face. You're...you're..."

She stopped herself, aware of how foolish she would sound if she blurted out what she was thinking. She might not know much about the world, thanks to her isolated upbringing, but even she knew that people didn't normally go around telling grown men they were beautiful.

She just couldn't get over the image of Haiden's face. He was younger than she'd realized, and there was no denying he was handsome. But it was more than that. His face was achingly dear, his features familiar when they had no right to be.

"What do you mean?" Haiden said roughly. "That's impossible."

She shook her head, his contradiction only making her more stubborn. "It's not. I saw you. It happened last night as well, but only for a moment. This time it was sustained. I could actually look at you."

Haiden was silent for a moment, his breathing slowing as he thought her words over. "Your magic," he said, his voice gruff. "You lifted the illusion enchantment. Temporarily, of course."

"Illusion enchantment?" Ember asked, pushing herself slowly to her feet. "What do you mean?"

Haiden seemed reluctant to respond, and Ember crossed her arms, pinning him with a stare and raising one eyebrow.

He sighed in concession. "My form hasn't actually changed. It only looks different."

"So you see your normal human self?" Ember asked, amazed. "When you look at your hand, or your body?"

Haiden shook his head, his lips stretched grotesquely

over his tusks. "I see the monster as well," he said quietly. "But I *feel* human when I touch things." He paused. "Most of the time."

"So if I sing, I can lift your enchantment?" Ember asked, eagerly. "I can fix it?"

Haiden shook his head again. "If it was that simple, don't you think I would have done it by now? I'm a singer, remember?"

Ember tilted her head to the side, regarding him. His monstrous features looked more ridiculous than ever, now she knew that they were simply concealing a very human face.

"I don't know," she quipped. "Maybe you don't want to lift it. Maybe you like having a boar face. You seem very intent on keeping everyone away, and those features must be helpful in that goal."

"If only," Haiden said dryly, although she thought his lips twitched a little. "It hasn't slowed down the stream of would-be rescuers." He gave her a pointed look. "It didn't keep you out, either."

"Yes, well, monsters don't scare me all that much," Ember said brightly. "My lack of fear turned my parents gray before their time, honestly." She studied him. "I still think I should try it. I lifted the enchantment for a moment, didn't I?"

Haiden grunted. "No, you didn't. You just saw through it. You used your own magic to counteract the illusion enchantment's effect momentarily. You didn't break or remove the curse. And even what you did was only temporary."

"Maybe I could make it permanent if I learned to sing better," Ember argued.

"Honestly, I doubt it," said Haiden. "I suspect it was a

lucky accident that your magic did something so targeted on your first attempt to channel it. It will take you a while to learn to get it to do what you want it to."

"I'm a fast learner," Ember said stubbornly.

"I don't care how fast a learner you are, Ember," said Haiden exasperated. "You can't sing constantly so as to continuously counteract the illusion enchantment."

Ember considered this. "But there must be a way to craft magic to do something even when I'm not singing. Your door is magically protected, and you're not constantly singing."

"True," Haiden acknowledged. "You can learn to create enchantments, a bit like the enchantments elves craft into talismans. But those don't last forever. They need to be renewed regularly. And they take a great deal of finesse, which you're a long way off mastering."

Ember took no offense from the accurate assessment of her ability.

"But if I did master that finesse, would there be a way to craft an enchantment powerful enough to last forever? Or at least, for a very long time? One that could counteract your illusion enchantment even if I'm not present?"

Haiden was silent for a long moment before answering. He seemed surprised by her question, although she couldn't imagine why.

"You have a quick mind," he said at last, as if making a concession. "There are ways for singers to fuel enchantments constantly. But that's core magic, way beyond your level, and far too dangerous anyway."

"Why is it dangerous?" Ember demanded.

Haiden made an irritated noise in his throat. "You ask too many questions."

"And you don't give enough answers," she countered. "Why is it dangerous?"

"Because it's constantly connected to the singer who cast it. Specifically, to their heart," Haiden said curtly.

"Which means...?" Ember prompted.

"Which means it creates a link between the singer who formed the enchantment and the subject of the enchantment. The singer fuels it constantly, their energy being drained by it every day. And unless broken, it continues until the singer's heart stops."

Ember frowned thoughtfully. "You've made it sound very dramatic," she said. "But how much does it really drain the singer's energy? When I used magic just now, I didn't feel tired at all. I think I'd be willing to at least try it."

"Then you'd be a fool," said Haiden, growing angry for no reason Ember could see. "And an arrogant fool to think that you could pull it off. It would probably kill you, because you'd have no hope of doing it correctly. And it would gain what? An artificial counteracting of an enchantment that would still be in place on me? Core magic isn't beginner work, Ember. Just leave it alone."

"But—"

"I didn't ask for your help," he said, almost shouting now. "I certainly didn't ask you to take risks for me. I'm fine without any help."

And before Ember's bewildered eyes, he turned and strode into the hut, slamming the door behind him.

# CHAPTER TWELVE

## Haiden

Haiden leaned back against the door, closing his eyes for a pained moment. He knew he'd been rude, and behaved childishly. But why did Ember never know when to leave well enough alone? She had such a knack for finding the topics that would most rattle him. It was incredible how quickly her mind had jumped to the more advanced possibilities magic presented. She was obviously both intelligent and perceptive.

And terrifying in a way he'd never experienced before.

As unsettled as he'd been by her questions about core magic, it didn't compare to the alarming and overwhelming experience of her fingers finding his face. He could still feel their warmth, the sensation almost painful even now, as though a burning brand had been applied instead of a gentle touch. No one had tried to touch him in five years. Not even a casual brush.

He should have realized what was happening. He'd recognized that something had been strange, locked as he was in the intensity of her gaze, but it hadn't been until afterward that he'd identified what it was. She'd been looking at his face, his actual face, instead of a spot above his head.

There could be no doubt she'd truly seen him. What had she made of the real him? She certainly hadn't shied away.

Sensing how dangerously his thoughts were softening, Haiden forced a scowl onto his face. He'd do well to remember how interfering she was being. And how destructive to his peace of mind. After weakening his defenses with her unexpected touch, she'd somehow steered the conversation straight onto one of the touchiest topics he could have thought of.

Core magic.

But Haiden's anger couldn't last. He was too aware of how unreasonable it was. Ember had no way of knowing that core magic was a tortuous obsession of his. How could she guess that this type of magic had defined his childhood? He'd been disappointed it wasn't taught at the academy, and spent hours in his own research, sometimes from less than reputable sources. He thought he had a better understanding of core magic than most singers on the continent. And the idea of Ember—a singer with literally no experience—contemplating this volatile, dangerous use of magic for the questionable benefit of Haiden looking less scary to strangers was too absurd to be anything but humorous.

And yet, he wasn't laughing. The emotions stirring in his heart were of a different type altogether. Why was she so willing to take risks for him, when she had no reason to care about his welfare? It made no sense. And he would never let her do it. Not even if it could actually lift the curse instead of just counteracting its effect. He wasn't that much of a monster.

A soft sound caught his ears, and he pushed away from

the door, turning so as to better listen. Ember was trying to sing again. Haiden couldn't help smiling at her less than melodic attempts. But considering she'd had no chance to experiment with her craft during her childhood, it was impressive how quickly she was picking it up. And she clearly had the determination—something harder to teach.

Thoughts of teaching shamed Haiden. He'd agreed to train her in songcraft, and yet he'd abandoned her to struggle on alone as soon as she'd achieved the tiniest measure of success. He needed to pull himself together and stop making everything so personal. She'd come to free her island, not to dig into his past or try to change his current circumstances.

He pulled the door open, assuming an untroubled demeanor and trusting that Ember simply wouldn't bring up his display of temper.

"Come out of your sulks, have you?" she asked him cheerfully.

He should have known better.

Smiling in spite of himself, Haiden rolled his eyes. "Apparently I have. Now come on. There's a lot to learn if you want to use your songcraft to help free your island."

Ember brightened. "Do you really think I can do that?"

"I don't see why not," said Haiden. "If you're the first singer in generations, you have power no one else does. The leaders only have power because they've convinced everyone that they do." He waved vaguely at his face. "It's much like this illusion enchantment. It affects what people perceive, but not the reality."

"I don't know about that," said Ember ruefully. "Their power feels pretty real when you're there."

"And this face looks pretty real to every child who's run screaming from me in the last five years," Haiden said. His voice was dry, but he injected a serious note into it. "I can already see how much promise you have, Ember. Your leaders are just manipulators. You're the one with the power to actually change things."

With the words, he let his voice morph into song, calling magic up from the ground and into himself. In the way he'd been taught, he didn't release it straight away, letting it pool inside him until he felt full to bursting. Then he urged his voice higher, singing a tribute to growth and life, to roots and foundations. At the edge of the clearing, a small tree began to shake, leaves drifting from its rustling branches. He saw Ember watching in fascination as the tree was pulled from the ground, shifting upward until roots and all were dangling free.

Directing it with his song, Haiden sent it a foot away from the gaping hole it had left, his song dropping and becoming gentler as he caused the roots to reach down into the ground, burrowing themselves in and seeking a new home.

A minute later, the tree went still, only a few branches waving gently as it settled into its new position.

"That was amazing," Ember said breathlessly, as soon as his song ended.

Haiden had to restrain a boyish grin, enjoying her admiration far too much. His own breaths were coming quickly, his energy depleted by the enormous effort it took to move an entire tree. It was a foolish enchantment to choose, a showy trick that demanded a great deal and achieved very little. But it was certainly satisfying to see Ember's hazel eyes wide with wonder. She had very expressive eyes, he'd noticed.

"Can you teach me to do that?" Ember pressed, turning those eyes to him.

Haiden chuckled. "We might have to build our way there," he said. "But yes, I can teach you."

In fact, he admitted to himself, he was very much looking forward to doing it.

Haiden spent the rest of the day pushing Ember as hard as he thought she could handle. Her eagerness to learn her songcraft made her a very attentive pupil. He could tell that all she wanted was to sing, but every time he had to stop her to explain the theory behind what she was trying unsuccessfully to achieve, she made no complaints. She just listened with a rapt attention that was both gratifying and unnerving after years of people trying not to look directly at him.

By the end of the day, they were both exhausted, and Haiden had gained a new appreciation for his instructors back at the academy. Teaching someone else songcraft—especially someone with absolutely no experience in it—was harder than he would have guessed.

There was no doubt Ember had the gift. She could sense the magic in the ground, and could now reliably pull it up into herself. That part was instinctive for singers, something most understood without being taught from the first time they found their voice.

Mastering how to mold that magic and release it to a specific purpose was a different matter altogether. That skill would take time, and Haiden was very aware of the risks uncontrolled magic posed to singers who didn't have the experience to handle it safely. And to all humans, really. In the forest where he'd grown up, the magic in the ground had grown so thick and dangerous it threatened to drive non-singers out, given they couldn't safely withstand the attempts of magic to rise up into their bodies. Usually magic wasn't so pushy as to try to force its way in—that was why singers had to pull it from the ground on purpose. But when the ground became as clogged with magic as it had been in his forest, it started to go wild. If it had gone far enough, then walking the forest floor would have been as lethal to a non-singer as passing through a barrier of pure magic, like the one that had turned Haiden back from his attempt to sail to the Reviled Lands.

He stilled, his mind trying to find a thread in these thoughts that was eluding him.

"Did I do it wrong?" Ember's voice pulled him from his reverie. "It seemed to work—I felt the magic swirl up and out of me—but you seem disapproving."

"No, you did it correctly," Haiden assured her. "I was thinking about something else."

"What?" Ember cocked her head to one side, sweeping a disheveled red curl out of her eyes.

"I don't see how my thoughts are any of your business," Haiden said, the surliness more a matter of habit than reflective of his current mood.

"I'm sure you don't, but I think you know by now that I'll just badger you until you make it my business, so you may as well give in early and save us both the effort," Ember replied cheerfully. She'd yet to be daunted by any grumpiness of his.

He sighed. Confound her, she was right.

"I was thinking about the barrier over the ocean. The one you felt but passed through unscathed—presumably because you were sailing *away* from your island—and I got turned back by." His frown deepened. "It was certainly strong magic."

"What did it feel like?" Ember asked.

She seated herself on a stump with the air of one very glad for a break. Haiden didn't blame her.

"Like pure agony," he said shortly. "Like the magic was trying to rip me apart."

Ember considered this. "That sounds awful. What damage did it do to you?"

"Well...it's hard to know," Haiden admitted. "Because reaching the barrier also triggered the elf's curse. So I don't know what was caused by the barrier and what by his curse. But when the pain dissipated, I suppose my body was perfectly functional."

Ember studied his face, clearly aware that there was more behind the words. "What are you thinking, Haiden?"

The soft, direct question, and especially the casual use of his name, had the same inconvenient effect on Haiden that he'd started to expect. Why he found it so difficult to say no to her—no matter how impudent her impositions might be—he couldn't explain to himself. He recognized it as weakness, even dangerous weakness. And yet, most alarming of all, he found himself eager to give in to it.

"I'm wondering if the barrier isn't a targeted attack so much as a solid wall of magic. One that's been pointed toward the mainland. That would probably be easier to set up than an enchantment that actually had to mold that volume of magic with any finesse. But it would still be lethal for most people to pass through if they were going the wrong direction."

"Most people?" Ember repeated.

"Well..." Haiden hesitated, reluctant to continue when he knew he was only speculating. He didn't like to make a claim that might later be proven wrong. Overinflated pride, perhaps, but he'd yet to find the secret to letting go of it. "If it was just a concentrated barrier of magic, it shouldn't be fatal for a singer. It might be painful, and it would undoubtedly be dangerous to have that much magic try to enter the singer's body. But it shouldn't actually kill them."

"Interesting." Ember's hazel eyes were gleaming, and Haiden felt a shot of unease.

"At least, it shouldn't kill an experienced singer," he added. "One without the proper training could probably be overwhelmed by it."

Ember didn't respond. Her eyes were drifting eastward, toward the ocean, and she seemed lost in her own thoughts.

"I think that's enough for today," Haiden said abruptly. "You'll learn better tomorrow on a full night's sleep." He glanced up at the sky, which was slowly darkening. The sun had dipped behind the treetops now. "I'll check the traps. We might be able to manage fresh meat for dinner."

"I can come with you," Ember offered.

Haiden shook his head. He'd put new enchantments in place after Ember's second attack, under the guise of demonstrating songcraft for their training. He couldn't explain why he felt such a powerful urge to protect her, but the fact remained that he didn't care to test how far from the dwelling they reached.

Not that he admitted as much. "I don't need help," he said instead.

Ember gave him a look. "So you keep telling me. Well, I'll start some water boiling in case there's something to cook."

He looked at her doubtfully. "Do you know how to light a fire without magic?"

Ember laughed over her shoulder, already tripping lightly toward the building.

"Well, you'd hope so, since I certainly don't know how to light one *with* magic."

"How am I supposed to know?" Haiden said. "Maybe you've always just sat around letting other people light the fires and do the heavy lifting for you."

"Life on the island isn't like that." Ember still seemed amused as she paused in the doorway of the hut. "Everyone has to do their part. I may not have been trained to defend myself from attackers—clearly a catastrophic oversight—but I've been working hard all my life, and I'm far from helpless."

Haiden nodded. "Good. Build the fire the old-fashioned way. Don't try anything fancy with magic. I don't want my home burned down."

"Well, it's my home too, at present, so you can be sure I won't take any risks."

Ember had spoken matter-of-factly, but when Haiden didn't respond, her eyes darted to his face, showing a rare sign of self-consciousness.

"I'm sorry if that's overstepping. But this really is the only place where I have sanctuary on this whole continent. The only place I know."

Haiden shrugged. "It's fine."

The words were inadequate, but that was for the best. He didn't want to share what he was feeling. He didn't want to acknowledge even to himself how much it had warmed him to hear her refer to his poorly built, misshapen hovel as her home.

As Haiden checked the traps, his mind was full of Ember's progress during the day. He'd felt a pang of something like envy as he'd watched her enthusiasm grow with each small breakthrough. It would be...well, magical...to discover the joy of having his voice all over again. His own discovery, at only four years old, had been tainted by his mother's utter horror when she learned of it.

Or maybe that horror had been mainly because of the elf prophecy. Perhaps without that detail, she would have been softer toward her son's unexpected gift.

Probably not.

Haiden frowned at the first—empty—trap, lost in contemplation of his childhood and the prophecy that had shaped his life.

"Blasted elves," he muttered to no one in particular.

*You are an enemy indeed, young singer. You will bring down a rising kingdom.*

The elf princess hadn't comprehended how drastically her words would bring his world crashing down. But he didn't feel much softness toward her on that account. Her intentions hadn't been evil, but nor had they been good. Like most elves, she was simply unmotivated by human interests, one way or the other. It was a matter of indifference.

To most elves, anyway. Haiden's scowl grew as he thought of the elf who'd cast the illusion enchantment on him. That one was far from indifferent. Haiden had rarely seen an elf show such malice to the humans whom most considered beneath their notice.

He'd been very quick to leap to hatred when Haiden had insulted him. A foolish thing for Haiden to do, but he'd lost his own temper when the elf brought up that cursed prophecy.

And he was back to the prophecy.

Why did it still haunt him? Why did he still feel like some part of him was afraid of turning into the monstrous enemy his mother had believed all singers to be, including her own son? The prophecy was resolved now. The elf princess's words had been fulfilled back in Teren.

So why did the elf in Arville claim that it still hung about him?

Haiden completed the circuit, pleased to find one trap that had yielded results. The rabbit wasn't a lot, but it would be enough to give Ember energy for the next day's training. He didn't need much. He'd learned in childhood to make do with little food when occasion required. His thoughts strayed to his sister, far away in Terenford. She might live in luxury now, but she was as tough as any forester had ever been. She'd been the one to go without so he could eat, in those first terrifying years as two children living alone in a huge forest.

And how did he repay her? By slipping away like a thief in the night and sending her no word of his welfare for five years.

Haiden let out a groan as he emerged from the tree line into the clearing. Why was he so sentimental and maudlin today? He didn't want to think about his childhood, or his abandoned family responsibilities. Ember was undoubtedly to blame. Her utter dependence on him—and even more so, her artless willingness to acknowledge it—stirred something within him that had been dormant for a long time. Something that caused him to look in the mirror and not like what he saw.

And the monstrous boar's features had nothing to do with that reaction.

# CHAPTER THIRTEEN

# Haiden

Haiden entered the hut to see Ember coaxing a fire into life under a pot full of water. She hadn't been lying about her capabilities, then. She turned when he opened the door, beaming at him with such cheerfulness his spirits lifted. He should be resentful to be welcomed into his own house by an intruder, but he wasn't.

"You found something!" Ember cried. "Do you need me to prepare it?"

Haiden raised an eyebrow. "Is skinning and gutting animals one of your talents?"

"Of course," said Ember matter-of-factly. "Chickens more often than rabbits. Still, I do know how." She held out her hand, but Haiden shook his head.

"No, I can do it."

To his surprise, Ember followed him outside, sighing in apparent satisfaction as she took in the first few stars beginning to appear in the dusky sky. For someone adrift in the world with nowhere to go, no plan for her future, a homeland that was trying to kill her, and an unknown enemy targeting her even here, she was certainly a cheerful person.

What had her prospects been like back on her island that her current situation felt like such an improvement?

"You said you've worked hard all your life," he asked abruptly. "At what? Are your parents farmers? Fishermen?"

Ember shook her head. "My father is a miner. But many on the island are farmers and fishermen. I didn't go into the mine with him, but my mother and I had plenty to do. We kept a few animals just for our needs, and did some other things, like sewing and mending, to help make ends meet." A strange look came over her face. "I was going to be a farmer though, or at least a farmer's wife."

"What?" Haiden demanded, taken aback by this confession.

Ember nodded. "My parents had arranged a match for me with a farmer. Gil. My future was all laid out before me." Her solemn expression suddenly gave way to a grin. "But fortunately I was chosen to be sacrificed to the monster instead."

Haiden wasn't sure how to react to this information, so chose a safer topic. "What does your father mine?"

"The same thing as every miner on the island," said Ember. "Regal onyx. It's a precious stone, and it's very beautiful. We use it as currency, among other things."

Haiden grunted, his eyes on his task as he prepared the rabbit. "I've never heard of it. But then, I don't know anything about mining or precious stones. On the mainland, that's the province of elves."

"Yes, well, we don't have them on the island," Ember pointed out. "So humans do the mining. But I'm not surprised you haven't heard of regal onyx. It's only found on the island, or so I've always been told." He could hear the bitterness in her voice. "Not that I can trust anything I've ever been told, probably."

Haiden glanced at her, once again reluctantly acknowledging the stirring of emotion. This time sympathy.

"That must be hard."

Ember drew in a deep breath, her chest rising and falling slowly before she answered.

"It is hard. Unsettling. But...also freeing." She gave him a wry smile. "I was always a troublemaker on the island."

"Figures," he muttered, and her smile grew.

"I didn't like to just accept what I was taught. There was always this lingering feeling that things didn't add up, as everyone else seemed to think. Learning how much I was deceived means I wasn't crazy all along, like they thought."

Haiden nodded. "I can understand that. Nothing someone else says or does to us can shake us as deeply as the things we find in our own hearts."

Ember was silent for long enough to make Haiden glance up at her curiously. It wasn't often she was at a loss for words.

"The things we find in our own hearts," she repeated, so softly she seemed to be speaking to herself. She looked up, saw him watching her, and added more naturally, "I wanted to ask you about something you said when I told you what I'd thought singers were."

"What did I say?" Haiden asked warily.

"You said that singing doesn't relate to the capacity to kill another human." She hesitated, then hurried on. "But you said that every human being has the capacity to kill another."

"Yes." Haiden paused his task, giving her his full attention. Clearly her question had been playing on her mind for a while. "I don't think anyone is immune to it."

"That troubles me," said Ember.

"Why?" Haiden asked.

She grimaced at him. "Because it means *I'm* not immune to it."

Haiden chuckled. "I don't think you're likely to give in to those darker impulses, Ember. You're too..." He waved the hunting knife in an unintentionally gruesome gesture. "Too cheerful."

Ember laughed at that. "Can't cheerful people do terrible things, then? Is it only surly, grouchy, unsociable misers like yourself?"

Haiden shrugged. "If you have the label anyway, may as well live up to it."

Ember let out a snort that brought a grin from Haiden. He couldn't imagine any of his would-be maiden rescuers betraying themselves with such a sound.

"Your tough talk doesn't fool me for a moment," she informed him sternly. "You're as soft as lamb's wool underneath that hideous visage and all that sarcasm."

"I'm no such thing," said Haiden, outraged.

Ember gave him a speaking look. "Then why haven't you killed me yet, when I've continued to intrude on your peace?"

"There's a lot of space between killing those who annoy you and being as soft as lamb's wool," Haiden protested.

"But you haven't even harmed me," Ember pointed out. "You bound my wounds when I was helpless and unconscious. You saved my life twice now, and let me sleep in your bed."

Haiden cursed his own foolishness as he heard his voice turn as gruff as a raw schoolboy's. "You didn't give me much choice."

"Nonsense," said Ember briskly. "You don't strike me as someone who's ever let others dictate your actions to you. Certainly not a freckled, helpless stranger who marched into your clearing with nothing but strong opinions to back her up."

Haiden cast a look over her innocent face. "You are very freckled," he said brutally. He nudged her exposed shoulder with his elbow.

"I know." Ember just grinned. "I like to be outdoors." She nodded toward his task as she added, "If you're still unconvinced, tell me this. What are you doing right now?"

"Gutting a rabbit with a sharpened blade," said Haiden blankly. "Is that an activity considered *soft* where you come from?"

Ember ignored his sarcasm. "You're not only providing food for me, but preparing it with your own hands, even though I offered to do it."

Haiden extended the bloodied knife toward her. "Fine, you want to do it?"

"I'm happy to," said Ember pleasantly, reaching toward the blade.

Haiden pulled it back before she could get her hands dirty, irritated that she'd called his bluff.

"Don't be ridiculous," he said, his voice surlier than ever.

Ember looked like she was trying not to laugh as she folded her hands demurely over her lap. "I feel my point has been made. The monster is a convenient face for you, but it bears no relation to who you actually are. I doubt it ever has."

That same warmth rose up in Haiden again, this time alarmingly strong. Its persistence scared him, and he felt an illogical anger come hard on its heels.

"You don't know anything about me," he said shortly. "If you construct some idealized image in your mind, making everyone you meet out to be a paragon of virtue just because you want to think well of people, then you're a fool who's setting yourself up to be disillusioned and betrayed."

"Not everyone." Ember shook her head, naively confident in her assessment of him. "Just you."

Haiden let out a noise of frustration. "Are you so quick to forget what we were just talking about? Everyone is capable of darkness, Ember. Everyone is capable of killing. Including me."

"So you claim," said Ember lightly.

Haiden slammed the knife down, irked that she was so determined to be oblivious.

"Do you want to know why I reacted when you asked about core magic?" he demanded.

Ember looked surprised at the offer of an unsought answer. "Yes, I do."

"Because I know all about core magic," Haiden went on, unsure himself why he was so riled up by Ember's praise. "I've experienced it. Someone used core magic on me when I was a child. Someone close to me. Someone I trusted."

"I'm sorry," said Ember, genuine compassion crossing her bright, open features. It only made Haiden more agitated.

"That was before I learned that only fools give their trust as freely as you do," he said darkly.

Ember said nothing.

"My sister was also affected," Haiden went on. "We suffered a great deal because of the magic used against us. When we learned what it was, we also learned that killing the person who did it would free us. A person who, in spite of what they'd done, was at that moment helpless and pathetic. A person no good man would consider harming."

Ember was still silent. The understanding in her eyes

suggested she had a pretty good guess who that person was, but she didn't ask him to say it aloud.

Haiden drew a breath. "My sister didn't hesitate for a moment to say that we'd never consider killing that person."

"And you?" Ember asked calmly.

Haiden's muscles were so tense, he could feel his arms shaking. When he spoke, his voice was nothing but a husky whisper. "I hesitated."

"And then?" Ember prompted. The stern note in her voice reminded Haiden of the most rigid of his instructors at the academy. It would have been comical if his mind hadn't been in such turmoil.

"And then I agreed that we wouldn't consider it," he said, his voice more natural. He paused, then pushed on, recklessly determined for her to know the truth of his heart. "But part of me was tempted. Even though I was little more than a child, part of me wanted to do it. And not just to be free. Also for revenge."

"But you didn't do it, did you?" Ember asked. "You didn't even attempt it?"

He shook his head mutely.

She clucked her tongue, her voice once again stern. "I'm amazed you can remember things so far back, when you apparently can't remember what you said to me mere days ago."

"What did I say now?" Haiden demanded.

"You said that although everyone has the capacity to kill, most choose never to do it, and that choice means more than if they only refrained because they were incapable."

Haiden said nothing, unable to argue with his own logic.

"You're not a monster because you were tempted, Haiden," she went on, her voice softer now. "Especially not when you were a child who'd been grievously wronged. You didn't give in to that temptation." Her voice turned dry. "If we were judged for one moment of hesitation, we'd all be doomed."

Still he was silent. Darkness had fallen now, but even in the moonlight Haiden could see Ember's forehead crease with concern. Why did she care so much about how he felt? It sent a pang of joy through him, one that was painful in its unfamiliarity.

"You should really believe me," she told him. "You think I know nothing of people. But it's just your world I know nothing about. I didn't grow up alone in a cave. I grew up surrounded by people just like the ones you know." She sighed. "They certainly weren't any more virtuous than those on the mainland, as I've discovered the hard way. Trust me when I say, Haiden, in spite of what you look like, there's nothing of the monster in you."

Haiden looked away, unable to take the intensity of her scrutiny, even if she was still looking at a spot over his head. He flexed his misshapen fingers before his eyes, feeling their sturdy, familiar strength. It was hard to believe that only a few days ago, he'd not only seen but felt the warping of his form. Everything felt very human now.

With the intuition he should really give her more credit for, Ember seemed to sense his need for a change in topic.

"Do you miss the forest where you grew up?" she asked, her tone returned to its normal lightness.

"Sometimes," said Haiden, picking the knife back up and continuing his work. "I'm not in any hurry to go back, though. My sister doesn't live in the forest anymore, and we never had a permanent home there that I'd want to return to." He smiled ruefully. "I mostly miss the fact that I belong to the land there, so to speak."

"I never suspected you of such sentimentality," Ember said.

He laughed. "Actually I was thinking practically. I miss being able to access the heart magic of that forest."

"What do you mean by heart magic?" Ember asked, intrigued.

"That's far beyond the beginner level we've reached in our theory today," Haiden pointed out.

"Oh, don't be so sour," Ember scolded him. "Just explain it, and I'll try to keep up."

Haiden shook his head, even as he knew he'd give in.

"Fine," he said, carrying the dissected rabbit inside with Ember trailing behind. "Heart magic is a deep form of magic. Or more like a deep source of the same magic that's in the ground everywhere. Those who have that connection to the land from which they're drawing the magic—a connection in their blood, their heart, or both—can get it to respond to them in ways it won't to an outsider."

"That's fascinating," said Ember, stirring the pot of water as he added the rabbit meat. "What does it allow you to do?"

"Depends on the land in question," said Haiden. "I'm not sure it's a concept that's understood everywhere. Or that even exists everywhere. The forest where I grew up is a particularly defined region, with its own ways, its own magical traditions, and very potent power in the ground. Someone growing up in a heavily populated city may never experience that same connection."

"I bet it exists on the island," Ember said, stirring absently. "It's more insular than any forest could be. And my people's connection to the land is deep. The island is everything to us. It's all we've had for generations."

"Maybe," said Haiden. "It's very possible, but I wouldn't

know."

He went outside to clean up, leaving Ember to take over the meal preparation. The domestic scene was entirely foreign to him, and yet comforting on a deep level. He thought he could get used to living that way, and the thought scared him.

Everything seemed to scare him lately, and he didn't like it.

His thoughts strayed to that morning, when Ember had seen past the illusion enchantment. It took a great effort of will not to reach up and touch the same place she'd touched on his face. Remembering that he hadn't yet cleaned his hands since preparing the rabbit helped.

But washing up couldn't distract him from the emotions wreaking havoc with his mind. However unintentional, it was an impressive feat for Ember to have seen through his illusion on her first use of magic. Apparently she was also convinced she could see through all his defenses and accurately assess the man he was underneath.

That part Haiden was more skeptical about. He couldn't remember ever feeling this kind of anxiety. Her opinion of him was too high. He was sure to let her down. Frustration rose up in him. He hadn't asked for this. He hadn't asked for her to form a good opinion of him, and in so doing, make him responsible for whatever disillusionment and destruction of trust would come when she inevitably realized how broken and flawed he was.

What right did she have to intrude on his peace this way?

And the worst of it was, he wasn't even the greatest threat to her. Someone—most likely the elf—was trying to kill her. He'd been too optimistic in thinking he could teach her to defend herself with magic in one day.

Haiden returned to the hut in a subdued frame of mind and spoke little throughout the meal. Ember didn't seem to mind. She was pleasant as usual, but he could see her flagging. She must be exhausted after spending the entire day using mental muscles she hadn't even known she had a short time ago.

When Haiden offered to clean up so that Ember could go straight to bed, she didn't protest. And by the time he returned to the hut from washing their bowls in the stream, she was already asleep.

Haiden hovered in the tiny dwelling, half guilty and half fascinated at the opportunity to study her unobserved. He hadn't really thought about it when she first forced her way into his clearing and his life, but he acknowledged now that Ember was beautiful. And all the more so because it wasn't a polished or intentional type of beauty. There was just a warmth about her, from her fiery hair and freckled shoulders to her ready smile. She glowed like the sun.

He grunted at his own nonsense. He'd become perfectly accustomed to the darkness, thank you very much. He'd had no desire to invite sunshine into his home.

Still...

He leaned down, shifting a wayward strand of hair with a hand that, while it looked repulsive, felt very human.

When he straightened up, it was with a renewed sense of determination. Just because he hadn't planned for Ember's flame to come into his life didn't mean he was going to let anyone snuff it out. Teaching her songcraft wasn't enough. He needed to confirm who was trying to kill her and stop them before they got through his defenses.

Making absolutely sure that his protective enchantments were still in place, Haiden slipped from the hut.

## CHAPTER FOURTEEN

# Ember

Ember woke to the pleasant sound of birdcall, her mind grasping her location immediately this time. She was in Haiden's hut, stealing his bed once again. She squinted toward the small window. It was properly morning, by the looks of it, which meant she'd slept very soundly. She'd been tired enough to sleep for a week.

Memory as to the reason for her exhaustion returned suddenly, and she sat upright. She was eager to get back into training. There was so much more to learn, and far too few hours in the day during which to learn it.

She pulled on her boots, realizing as she did so that the hut felt strange.

"Haiden?" she said his name softly, not wanting to wake him if he was still sleeping. He'd surely been worn out by the previous day's activities as well.

When there was no reply, she crept to the doorway into the next room. She could see the blankets where he'd slept, but the space was empty. No wonder the house felt different. There was a stillness to an empty home. She felt a strange sense of loss at the realization she was alone. Probably just because she'd never lived alone, she told herself. Not because she was so dependent on Haiden that she couldn't be without him for five minutes. He was probably just checking the traps.

She took advantage of the solitude to freshen up, wishing that she had a different gown to change into. The blue one was becoming dirty. She'd have to find an opportunity to wash it in the stream, and bathe while she was at it. How she'd manage that without a spare gown was a mystery.

Ember was just thinking about boiling water for breakfast when the door opened. Haiden appeared, water bucket in hand.

"Good morning," Ember said brightly. She held out her hands for the water. "It seems you read my mind." She paused as Haiden ignored her gesture and instead strode past her, filling the pot himself. "Hold on...that's not something magic can actually do, is it?"

Haiden snorted. "No, definitely not. Your thoughts are safe from me."

"Well, you're not safe from my thoughts," said Ember mischievously. "I don't really hesitate to share them."

"Yes, I've noticed that."

Haiden's voice was dry, but she didn't detect any actual annoyance. He did seem a little aloof, though, and Ember studied him surreptitiously as he stoked the fire. It was so hard to read his emotions with those boar features.

Quietly, Ember started to sing. She'd had the urge since the moment she woke, and giving in to it was like relieving pressure in her chest. She didn't bend down and touch the ground this time, as Haiden had gotten her to do the day before. She was encouraged to still feel the power stirring beneath her feet, a steady trickle soon drawing up into her.

She focused it on Haiden, her eyes narrowed with concentration, and was gratified to see the illusion flicker, revealing his handsome, albeit stern, face. It was only for a moment, but it was still encouraging. She was starting to get a feel for her craft. And if she could achieve these results here on the mainland, in terrain so foreign to her, what might she be able to do back on her island, with the possibility of heart magic at her disposal?

"What are you doing?" Haiden's voice was sharp as he turned his face toward her, his features decidedly monstrous again.

"Practicing," Ember said innocently.

He narrowed his eyes. "On me."

It wasn't a question, but Ember nodded anyway. "Who else am I supposed to practice on?"

"Magic doesn't have to be used on a person," groused Haiden.

"I need something useful to do," Ember told him. "I get into trouble when I'm at a loose end." Not taking no for an answer, she chivvied him away from the fire, assuming control over the preparation of food.

Haiden stood and watched her for a moment before retreating into the next room. Ember sang quietly to herself as she placed eggs into the pot of now-boiling water. She wasn't trying to do anything in particular with her magic, just practicing the sound.

"Do you have any more bread?" she called out, keeping her eyes on the eggs. When there was no answer, she prompted, "Haiden?"

Only a grunt greeted her words, the sound strained, as if Haiden was focusing hard on something. Curious, Ember moved to the doorway and peered into the second space.

She let out a scream at the sight of Haiden, poised with a blade against his own throat.

"Stop!" Ember flew across the room, her heart in her throat as she grabbed at Haiden's arm. Had she upset him so much with her invasion of his life?

But Haiden was already lowering the blade by the time her fingers closed around an arm that didn't match her vision at all.

"What are you doing?" he asked her blankly.

"What are *you* doing?" she demanded. "Why are you trying to slit your throat?"

"Slit my...?" Haiden trailed off, then let out a snorting laugh. "I'm not trying to slit my throat. I'm trying to shave."

"What?" Unconvinced, Ember maintained her grip on his arm. "The knife was against your neck."

"It wasn't," Haiden corrected her. "I'm under an illusion enchantment, remember? The form you see bears only the loosest connection to my actual body. My throat is here." He touched a spot that corresponded to the upper chest of his over-tall boar-like form. "This," he tapped the spot where the knife had been, "is actually my chin."

"Oh," said Ember, feeling foolish but also deeply relieved. "I thought I'd driven you over the edge."

A gleam of amusement shot through Haiden's eyes. "Not yet."

"What's the point of shaving if no one—including you—can see your face?" she asked reasonably.

"I could feel that I'm getting scruffy," Haiden shrugged. "It's uncomfortable."

"*Can* you even shave with the illusion enchantment in place?" Ember asked.

Haiden grunted. "It's challenging, but possible. I have to go by feel."

"Maybe I can help," said Ember.

"I didn't ask for your help," said Haiden, sounding irked.

"Don't be silly," she scolded him. "Let me just take the eggs off the fire." She bustled out then back in.

Raising her voice, she called magic forth from the ground, singing some nonsense words about power and enchantments. When she felt magic pass into her, she changed the song, telling the magic in so many words to counteract the enchantment illusion on Haiden. He'd explained the day before that while advanced singing didn't necessarily involve verbalizing what you wanted the magic to do, it was a good strategy for beginners as they learned to direct the power.

To her delight, the magic responded. Haiden's face flickered, then disappeared, his human features appearing at a lower spot that was still substantially above her own head. Still singing, she gestured excitedly to Haiden, who was looking surly rather than pleased. When he didn't respond, she grabbed his hand—his strong, human, well-formed hand—and raised it before his eyes.

"What are you doing?" he asked tersely, yanking his hand back. "Are you trying to break my curse? I didn't ask you to do that."

Ember let her song peter out, confused by his grouchy reaction. As soon as her voice went silent, his surly human features disappeared, replaced by the monster's face. "I thought you said your curse can't be broken just by singing at it," she said.

"It can't," Haiden confirmed shortly.

"So what are you getting worked up about?" she demanded. "I'm just trying to counteract the illusion, like I did previously. And it worked! Couldn't you see your real hand?"

Haiden shook his head. "It still looked the same to me. Like I told you, you're not removing the enchantment. You're just affecting yourself. Your song creates a shield around *you*, one that stops the illusion from working on you while it's up."

"Oh." Ember deflated, disappointed. "That doesn't really help you with shaving, does it?"

"I didn't ask for your help with shaving," said Haiden, still seeming unreasonably annoyed by her attempts to assist.

"You know what, if the illusion only disappears for me, I could do the shaving," said Ember, perking up. "My father taught me how, when he had an injury that prevented him from using his arm for a few weeks. Here."

Haiden protested as she attempted to take the knife. "It's not going to work. You won't be able to reliably direct the magic to do what you want. Not yet."

"It already worked," Ember protested, affronted. "I could see you perfectly." She flashed him a smile. "You're right— you are scruffy."

He didn't smile back. "If it worked, it was impressive, but most likely a lucky accident. It would take a strong singer to be able to bend magic to their will so soon after first finding their voice."

Ember just started singing again, confident that he was wrong. For whatever reason, this particular use of magic seemed to come more naturally to her than any other. Perhaps she had a gift for revealing what was hidden. She'd certainly been the only one to see through the masks everyone else accepted back on the island.

Sure enough, Haiden's face flickered back into sight as her words wound around him. She could almost feel them stripping back the layers of magic that coated his features. It was strangely reminiscent of the process she'd been undertaking since coming to the mainland, finding out information in trickles, allowing her to uncover the lies she'd been taught, layer by painful layer. With that image in mind, she urged the magic on, directing it to find all the hints of illusion about Haiden and pull them free. His face was revealed in perfect detail, his dark eyes and intense scrutiny causing her heart to stutter slightly.

Dipping the knife into the bowl of water Haiden had left on the table, she raised it to his face. It took all her concentration to keep the song going, and there was little focus left for the actual shaving. She placed her free hand along one side of his jaw, holding his face steady as she carefully moved the blade along his other cheek. She felt his jaw clench at her touch, and his whole body stilled. If he resented her intrusion into his space, however, he didn't say so.

Ember moved slowly along his jaw, working carefully as the sharp edge of the blade cut through Haiden's rough beard. After a minute, her concentration faltered, her song along with it, and the face before her started to flicker. She closed her eyes, letting the feel of Haiden's jaw under her fingers ground her in the reality of his true form. Her song swelled back around her, and she urged the magic to surround Haiden instead. She told it to settle on him, imagining it gathering in layers on his skin. She wanted it not to be solely dependent on her continuing to sing. She wanted to see his real face all the time. She found herself strangely desperate for it.

When she opened her eyes, his human features were clearly visible once again. The dark eyes that always had a slightly stormy look were fixed on her with such intense focus that it was hard to draw enough breath to continue her song. Forcing her gaze away from his, she focused once more on her task.

His face was half shaved now, and although he looked much neater on the shaved part, it almost seemed a shame. The dark hair still covering one half of his chin was bristly and rugged, but she didn't find the look unappealing. In fact, it suited him. There was an untamed quality about Haiden that she couldn't help but be drawn to. Certainly no one on the island had that quality about them. They were all proper and conforming. And yet, underneath, some of their hearts were as black as Haiden's was true.

Ember shifted the blade across to the other side of Haiden's face, her fingers shifting as well, to linger on the smoother skin where she'd already worked. His face felt warm, and again she could feel the tension in his jaw. The simple hut felt smaller and closer than ever before, Ember suddenly aware of the fact that she was pressed almost against a Haiden who now looked very much human. She didn't dare look up into his face again. The sensation of his eyes fixed on her was potent enough.

She finished her task, lowering the blade with a hand that wasn't as steady as it should have been. It wasn't the neatest shave, but it didn't really matter. No one but her was likely to see it.

A strange little surge of smugness went through her at the thought. She rather liked the idea that Haiden's face—all strong jaw, stormy brows and full lips of it—was a secret only she could access. She laid the knife on the table, realizing as she did so that she still had one hand resting on Haiden's face. Reluctantly, she went to pull it away, only to have Haiden's hand fly unexpectedly up to cover hers, trapping it in place.

Ember drew in a sharp, involuntary breath, her heart

seeming to stop in her chest at the contact. Although Haiden's jaw was still tense, his hand was warm and steady, no tremors in the strong fingers that held hers against his jaw.

Ember looked into his eyes at last, and the intensity of his gaze caused her voice to falter into silence. To her delight, Haiden's face remained visible. Some part of her—the newly found sense more developed than ever after a day of intensive training—recognized that the enchantment was still in place around Haiden. But her own crudely crafted enchantment was there as well, like a layer over the top of it.

These reflections flitted over her in a moment, but they fled before Haiden's sustained, silent regard. He was watching her with a focus she'd never encountered before. It was as though he saw right into her, and it was both heady and unsettling. She felt vulnerable, and the thought flashed through her mind that it would be nice to have a mask to hide behind, even a monstrous one. But she banished that foolish idea at once. She wasn't afraid to be seen, not by Haiden. She'd longed to be seen all her life, and had instead spent nineteen years trying to be less *herself* because what was inside her made those around her uncomfortable. She didn't feel that need with Haiden. She never had. Any more than she'd been afraid to see him, in any of his forms.

Ember could hardly think as Haiden's head dipped toward her. Her free hand seemed to have found its way to his chest, and he didn't push her away. On the contrary, his face was now so close to hers, she could see every patch she'd botched in her shaving attempt. Not that her eyes lingered long on those spots. She was too distracted by the way Haiden's eyes were flicking down her face.

Ember's eyes fluttered shut as his face drew close

enough that she could feel his breath. A tingle of anticipation passed over her as his nose brushed against hers, and she found herself leaning up on her toes.

The next moment, Haiden's hand was gone, and she could feel cold air rush between them. Ember opened her eyes, confused and embarrassed as she saw that Haiden had stepped back from her.

"All done," she said thickly, attempting to speak lightly as she nodded at his mostly clean-shaven jaw. "Much better."

Haiden didn't respond, just stared at her through heavily lidded eyes.

"You're welcome, by the way," Ember said, annoyed by his demeanor.

That got a reaction. "Am I supposed to thank you?"

"It is customary when someone helps you," Ember pointed out.

"I didn't ask for your help," Haiden said shortly. "I don't need it."

The anger lacing his voice was so ridiculous and such an overreaction to the situation that Ember knew it had to be a response to something under the surface. Clearly he'd been as unsettled by their moment of emotion as she had, although his instinctive response was very different from hers. Ember drew a deep breath, determined not to get offended. She would much rather understand what was happening inside him than defend herself.

She stepped closer to him again, her expression earnest. "Haiden, there's nothing wrong with letting people help you. Accepting help doesn't mean you're weak."

"I don't need your help," he growled again, retreating a step to recreate the distance between them.

"Accepting help doesn't necessarily mean you need

help," she insisted. "Sometimes it's just...nice to let someone help you."

Abruptly, Haiden stepped forward and grabbed her shoulders, the sudden movement startling her. His grip, so tight it was almost painful, was as human as ever, and thanks to her clumsy enchantment, his real face still showed as he leaned toward her.

"How many times do I have to tell you—I didn't ask for your help, and I don't want it!"

"Haiden," she said, rattled by the strength of his reaction. "It's all right."

Tentatively, she raised her hand. His features were flickering as her magic began to give way, and she closed her eyes as her questing fingers found the face she'd come to know. She stretched her fingertips lightly across his features, feeling how hard he was breathing.

"It's all right to be afraid," she whispered. "You haven't had to be human with anyone for so long. But you can trust me." When he didn't answer, she persisted. "You've let yourself believe you're a monster—that you deserve the face you wear. But your heart is good. I know it is."

For a pregnant moment Haiden was silent, his muscles feeling tense and his eyelids flickering shut against her touch. Then he pulled abruptly back from her, his voice savage.

"You don't know anything. And I'm not afraid."

Before Ember could catch her breath, he'd turned. She could only watch as he strode from the hut, his steps agitated. She moved to the door in time to see him disappear into the trees, leaving Ember feeling foolish and more alone than she had since the first moment she laid eyes on Haiden.

What had she done to deserve such a big reaction? Why

was he so sensitive to the idea of accepting her help? Why had it made him so angry every time he'd let her through his defenses?

But why shouldn't he be angry? He hadn't let her past his barriers willingly. She'd been forcing her way in since the moment they met. She'd consistently refused to be held at arm's length, ignoring his clear preference to be left to his own devices. There could be no question that she'd been imposing shamefully on him. She'd been eating his food, presuming on his time and effort to train her, even kicking him out of his own bed.

She felt ashamed. She'd been raised to be more considerate than that. And she shouldn't assume Haiden felt the same connection to her that she felt to him. Of course she felt a connection. He was quite literally the only person she knew on the entire continent.

"Enough," she told herself firmly. "More than enough."

She'd trespassed on his goodwill for too long. And in doing so, she'd lost sight of her whole purpose in seeking his help. She'd come back to his clearing determined to get assistance in freeing her island from the control of the Protector and his lies. Then she'd gotten so caught up in their two-person world, she'd lost sight of that goal. She hadn't even tried to find out what happened to the other girls who were supposedly sacrificed to the monster.

It was time for her to tend to her own business, and leave Haiden to his. In spite of Haiden assuring her that she was still a beginner, she felt infinitely more capable in songcraft than she had when they'd started their training.

Ember turned back into Haiden's poorly built hut. Her heart was in her throat at the thought of leaving, and even more so at the thought of never seeing Haiden again. But little as she wanted to return to the shackles of her island, she'd long since decided she couldn't take any other course with integrity.

She approached the little table, hunting for parchment to leave Haiden a note. Otherwise he might think she'd been snatched or something, and feel compelled to search for her. Her gaze found a stack of papers, and she drew them toward her. Scanning the words quickly, she paused. These were Haiden's notes on songcraft. She glanced at the window. It was still morning, and she had the feeling Haiden wouldn't be back for some time. She would probably be wise to take one last opportunity to learn what she could about her singing ability. She had no idea if she'd have another chance to learn from a singer.

Then, she would be on her way, and never trouble him with her problems again.

# CHAPTER FIFTEEN

# Haiden

Haiden strode blindly through the trees, his breaths coming far too quickly for the minimal exertion.

*You're a liar.*

The condemnation rang in his mind, cutting mercilessly into his whirling thoughts.

It was true, and he knew it. He'd told Ember he wasn't afraid, but he'd lied. She terrified him. She had since the moment he'd let her into his home and—an unfamiliar pang went through him at the thought—into his heart.

He couldn't afford to be vulnerable. He didn't *want* to be vulnerable. He much preferred the security of his solitude. In a flash of brutal honesty, he realized that a part of him liked the monstrous mask he wore. It was effective protection from most of the world. But for reasons he couldn't comprehend, it had never seemed to work on Ember.

She thought he had a good heart. But what did she know? What could the opinion of one naive girl, formed on the basis of his very half-hearted kindness, do against the destiny that had hung over him since childhood?

*You are an enemy indeed, young singer. You will bring down a rising kingdom.*

It was no use telling himself the prophecy had been resolved back in Teren. He'd tried to reassure himself with that lie for years. But if it had been resolved, he wouldn't still have been driven by the need to escape it all these years later. If it had been resolved, that cursed elf wouldn't have sensed its magic touch hanging around him when he first arrived in Arville.

Ember said he thought he was a monster, and maybe she was right. Hadn't he begun to sense his form actually changing, not just the appearance of it? Surely that was a sign that he was becoming the beast in earnest. The illusion enchantment was only supposed to affect what people saw, not his true form. If he was succumbing to it, that must be a reflection of what was in his heart.

But that had been before Ember came to stay with him. In fact, he'd felt the monster taking over his form when Ember had treated him like a monster. When she'd recoiled from his singing gift. He hadn't experienced it since she'd returned and cleared up her misconceptions about songcraft.

That was the heart of the matter, he acknowledged to himself. He'd spent his whole life trying, and still hadn't been able to escape the conviction his mother had created in him: that being a singer made him a monster.

It always came back to that. To outrunning his childhood.

Why had he told Ember anything about that old tale? Why had he admitted to the impulse that had once made him consider killing? Why had he shared any part of a past he'd sooner forget?

He knew she'd been referring to the previous night's confidences when she told him that he was wrong to think himself a monster. Her words had made him feel exposed, and the knowledge that it was all his own doing didn't soften his anger at all.

Why couldn't she leave him be? Try as he might, he hadn't been able to outrun the elf princess's prophecy. But at least her intentions hadn't been evil.

The elf in Arville was a different matter altogether, and Haiden was determined not to bow to that elf's malicious predictions. The vile creature had said that Haiden wouldn't be able to break the curse and would have to depend on someone else for help. But Haiden would never accept that, would never accept that the elf had the right to dictate his life as another elf had once done. Even if Ember had been capable of breaking the curse—which he was sure she wasn't—Haiden couldn't accept her help and in so doing, doom himself to once more be nothing but a puppet on a string. He *had* to take control of his own destiny, whatever it cost him.

*Whatever it costs you?* That brutally honest voice whispered in his head. *Even if it means you lose Ember? Is that a cost you're willing to pay?*

Haiden ignored the thought, trying desperately to turn his thoughts in another—any other—direction. He'd wandered far into the copse by now, and he urged his steps onward. He wouldn't be heading back to his hut until he had his emotions well under control.

He hadn't headed toward Arville—his attempts to find answers there the night before regarding the men who'd attacked Ember had been fruitless enough. Thankfully, this time, he didn't pass another soul in his tortured ramblings.

He wandered for hours before his turmoil had cooled enough to think about heading home. And by then he was a long way from his hut. As he got his bearings, reality came trickling back in. He realized he was hungry and weary, and also that he'd lost a whole day in which he'd promised to train Ember.

He started to feel anxious as he picked up the pace. He'd left Ember alone for many hours. And he'd been harsh to her when he left. Still, however bruised her feelings were, she would be safe if she stayed in the clearing, better yet if she stayed in the hut. Surely she would have the sense to stick within the magical protections. Wouldn't she?

Twilight was falling when Haiden finally reached the clearing. All was still and calm, but he knew at once that something wasn't right. He found himself surging across the open ground, throwing his door open with something close to panic.

"Ember?"

He didn't need the silence to tell him she wasn't there. Her absence screamed at him as jarringly as a hawk's shrill cry.

His panic grew as he spotted a folded piece of paper on his table. Haiden flicked the note open, his heart thudding painfully in his chest.

Haiden,

Sorry not to say goodbye in person, but I thought it was probably best not to delay. I'm returning to my island. Thank you very much for giving me shelter, and for all you've taught me. I truly do appreciate it.

I know I still have a lot to learn, but I really think you've taught me enough to help my people. Especially once I'm back on the island and hopefully have access to the heart magic of the land.

Haiden paused for a moment, groaning as he closed his eyes. Ember had no idea of the nuances of magic. Heart magic was complex and advanced, and not necessarily any use to her. She'd obviously understood it as a simple amplifier of either skill or potency of magic, but that wasn't the case. There was no way she was ready to face the monsters who'd so skillfully controlled a whole community for decades. Drawing a shaky breath, he read on.

I'm sorry for how much I've imposed, and I hope you'll find the peace you're looking for. You really have been very kind to me, don't let your critical self believe any different. I will always be glad and grateful that we met.

Yours,

Ember

Haiden stared at the final words for far too long, immobile and numb. *Yours, Ember.* If only she was his. An agonizing ache rose up in him as he was suddenly seized by the certainty that she *was* his. Or at least, she was supposed to be. But he'd driven her away, and might never see her again. In his surly fit of temper, he'd pushed her out, quite possibly to her own death.

His eyes fell on the parchments strewn across the table further along, and he snatched at them. His notes. She must have been reading them. A fresh wave of alarm washed over him as he realized that his notes about core magic were on top. What was in her mind? Did she think she could harness that deepest and most dangerous type of heart magic? She'd be mad to try. Even he'd never dared.

To be fair, he'd never found a cause that had made him even consider taking the risk. His interest in it had been more in the nature of understanding his past rather than planning for any future endeavors.

But Ember...it didn't take much thought to recognize that she would think saving her island was a cause worthy of using this dangerous type of magic. She wouldn't be deterred by the knowledge that even if she succeeded, she would be permanently draining herself of energy and, eventually, life. What would she do? Try to bind the leaders of the island with magic from her own core? Try to magically lift the deception placed over the rest of the community?

These things were far beyond Ember's level of ability. Far beyond those of most trained and experienced singers. She wouldn't succeed in her goal. But she would get herself killed trying. And that was if she even made it as far as the island. He should never have told her his theory that the barrier might only be fatal to non-singers. He had no idea if that was true, and she was going to gamble her life on it.

Of course, she might not even get as far as that, he realized. The malicious elf was still out there, bent on eliminating her in order to keep her island a secret. How many hours had she already been outside the protection of his clearing?

Fear swirled through him, its potency mocking his earlier confession to himself that he'd lied when he told Ember he wasn't afraid. He'd thought Ember terrified him, but it was nothing to the fear he felt now.

No.

He couldn't allow her to run blithely to her death. He had to go after her.

He was out the door before the thought had fully formed. He no longer felt the hunger that had chased him homeward, or the weariness from his day of wandering. There was nothing in his mind but Ember.

Darkness had fallen by the time Haiden reached Arville and burst into the tavern, taking no heed of the usual hush created by his appearance.

"Where is she?" He strode up to the bar, slamming one hand onto the counter.

The barkeep stared at him in astonishment, pausing midway through pouring a drink.

"Where's who?"

"Ember!" Haiden said impatiently. "The girl who worked for you a few days ago."

The man looked at him for long enough that Haiden was sure he was deciding what answer to give, rather than genuinely ignorant.

"Tell me," Haiden growled.

"I'm not sure I should," said the barkeep, showing what Haiden supposed was admirable courage. "You don't look fit to be trusted around a defenseless young woman."

"She's not defenseless," said Haiden, affronted on Ember's behalf. But he took a breath, allowing his temper to cool. "And I don't mean her any harm. I'm trying to stop her getting herself killed."

Still the barkeep didn't respond, and Haiden leaned forward over the bench, his voice softening.

"Please tell me what you know."

"Are you asking for my help? There's a once-in-a-lifetime marvel." The man looked amused, and Haiden pulled back in irritation. "No, no, don't get all offended," the barkeep admonished him. "Don't take yourself so seriously." He finished pouring the drink, sliding it along the bar to one of the many interested onlookers. "I haven't seen her, but word is she was down at the wharf today. Trying to barter passage on a boat heading eastward."

"And?" Haiden asked, pained.

"Who's going to take her east?" scoffed someone at a nearby table. "She was told the same thing you were told when you asked the same question all those years ago."

Haiden almost groaned. And she'd no doubt had the same reaction he'd had. That if no one would take her, she would have to go on her own. The question was, had she managed somehow to procure a boat?

"So where is she now?" he asked.

"Dunno," shrugged the man at the table. "Don't think she came back up from the wharf."

She'd found a way. Haiden was sure of it. She was the most determined person he'd ever met. Well, except perhaps for his stubborn self. He had to go after her.

The thought made him pause. He could chase her, no question. He'd be able to get hold of a boat. But would he catch her in time to stop her reaching the island? It was doubtful, if she had as big a head start on him as he suspected. Not to mention how easily he could miss her in the ocean. It wasn't like following a trail on land.

He needed to think more strategically. If he was too late to stop Ember from sailing eastward, then he needed to think further ahead, to what help she might need when she actually reached her island.

He refused to think *if* she reached her island.

"Where's the elf?" He turned back to the barkeep.

The man looked taken aback at the abrupt change in topic. "What do you mean?"

"You know what I mean. The elf who hangs around here, the one who cursed me. Where is he?"

"How should I know?" The barkeep wasn't quite meeting his eye.

"Don't be coy with me," Haiden said irritably. "Sooner or later, you know everything that happens in this town. You must know something about where he spends his time, or who would know where to find him."

"Even if I did, what benefit would it be to me to tell you?" the barkeep asked.

Haiden swallowed his impatience and frustration, knowing they wouldn't speed up the process. He didn't even try to be intimidating, or make use of his supposed extra height. "How about the benefit of knowing you might be helping to save Ember's life?"

It was a different approach for him, and he was a little surprised how effective it was. After regarding him for a long moment, the man let out a huff of air and nodded.

"He always comes into town along the coastline, from a northerly direction. Rumor is he has some kind of dwelling in the old quarry."

"Thank you," said Haiden sincerely. "I'm grateful."

"I'm not helping you for your sake," the barkeep said dryly. "Call me an old fool, but I've a soft spot for that girl."

"So much the better," said Haiden. "And you're not a fool—I think she has that effect on everyone she meets."

The barkeep looked much too interested in this declaration, but Haiden was already halfway across the room.

"You won't be able to just stroll in there!" the barkeep called after him. "Paranoid little critter like that, be sure he'll have some kind of protections up!"

Haiden just waved a hand in acknowledgment as he pushed his way through the doors out into the brisk night. Whatever magic the elf had in place, Haiden would be ready for it. There'd been no need to say as much to Ember, but he was strong by the standards of singers. Very strong, if his instructors at the academy were to be believed. It likely came from growing up in the magic-rich environment of the Forest of Ilgal. And he'd never been so full of energy and determination. With Ember's life on the line, he felt like he could overpower anything.

The walk to the quarry took the better part of two hours. The moon was riding high among sparse clouds, and the night was cold by the time Haiden reached the edge of the rocky area. Local word was that someone had found some kind of precious stone here early in Arville's settlement, and had excitedly opened mining operations. But it had proved to be a small and isolated vein, and no more was ever found. The mine was soon abandoned, and the town had reverted to its original industry of fishing.

Haiden had never actually heard what the precious stone was, and it now occurred to him to wonder if it was the one Ember had talked about. The one supposedly only found on her island. What had she called it? Regal onyx.

These unimportant details fled Haiden's mind as he climbed over the edge of the quarry. A large hole yawned before him, descending in layers in the moonlight. It was large enough that it would take a long time to search the whole area. But Haiden had a feeling he wouldn't need to.

He closed his eyes, humming softly to help bring his extra sense into focus. He could feel ripples of magic respond to him from the ground below, curling in invisible tendrils around his ankles and up his legs. He sent them outward cautiously in a seeking motion, weaving around them a complicated enchantment he'd perfected at the academy. It should shield the magic he was using from detection.

Sure enough, the questing power met its likeness, the clash of the two streams of magic sending back a jolt that jarred Haiden. Moving stealthily, he followed the direction of his stream. That was where the magical protections were found, and it was no doubt where the elf would be found as well.

It led him down into the quarry and through a tunnel, the entrance of which had been completely concealed from above. Haiden didn't have far to go before he could sense the presence of magic without even relying on his seeking song. And if that hadn't been a giveaway, the burning torches placed along the tunnel were.

He let his voice drop away, gathering strength for his next task. He'd reached the elf's nest now, but that was only the first step. Finding the magical protections wasn't the same as getting through them, and from the feel of it, the dwelling was coated in magic.

"Come to beg again, have you?"

The high voice made Haiden whirl, his heart hammering. He'd been foolish to assume the elf was inside his home. He should have done a better scout of the area before blindly following the magic. Now the creature stood between Haiden and the way out, blocking him in with every appearance of confidence.

# CHAPTER SIXTEEN

# Haiden

"You're wasting your time if you've come to beg," the elf informed Haiden coldly. "My answer hasn't changed."

Haiden said nothing, too busy letting out a near-silent song designed to gather power into himself and hold it in readiness. Singing too softly for detection was one of the skills they taught in advanced classes at the academy.

"That won't work," said the elf, his mocking tone reminding Haiden that elves had much better hearing than humans. "If you try to force me to help you, it won't count." He smirked, the expression rendering his face more inhuman in the flickering light of the torches. "Is it the girl? Has she made you want to be human again? Pathetic, like the rest of your kind."

"Where is she?" Haiden growled.

But the diminutive creature raised an eyebrow. "Left you, has she? More sense than the other girls, it seems." His expression grew more smug. "You're welcome for the company, by the way. I thought you might be lonely in your isolation. It's amazing how powerfully rumors of wealth and magic will work on the weak minds of young human girls."

Haiden breathed a secret sigh of relief that the elf was apparently not behind Ember's disappearance. He didn't waste time in trading more insults. He felt full to bursting from the power he'd drawn into himself, and keeping it bottled inside was a challenging discipline that he wouldn't be able to maintain for much longer.

Giving no indication of his intention to act, Haiden suddenly released his voice. He sent a barrage of magic toward the elf, crafting it into a freezing power.

With a cry, the elf sprang into motion, his long fingers delving into a pocket and emerging with a round golden disc, similar to a coin. Magic streamed out of the talisman, forming a bubble of protection around him. Haiden's initial assault bounced invisibly off it, but he wasn't daunted. He had plenty more energy to keep fighting, and he could feel the magic beneath his feet, seemingly clamoring for release. It was more potent down in the quarry than on the surface, which was most likely why the elf had settled there.

He sent another barrage at the little creature, crafting this one more skillfully, so that it separated into sharpened prongs that stabbed at the shield of power that still surrounded the elf. The protection wouldn't last much longer.

Haiden could see the elf's eyes widen in shock and alarm, and he felt a vicious satisfaction. His miniature adversary had never had reason to suspect the strength of Haiden's ability, or the level of control his training had given him over his magic. He'd never had cause to show it, and had thought it prudent to let the elf think him weaker or more raw than he was. But now was the time to use everything he had.

The shield was weakening, almost gone. Haiden could see that the elf was reaching for another talisman, but a shard of Haiden's attacking magic broke through just in time. Swiftly, Haiden changed the direction of his song, renewing the freezing enchantment he'd started with. The elf's arm froze in the act of reaching for another pocket, his eyes wide with fury.

Haiden didn't waste breath on taunts or threats. His voice was better used in continuing to sing, which he did with gusto as he strode forward. He might not truly have the form of the huge boar-like beast, but his human body was plenty strong enough to overpower the elf. He grabbed the creature by the throat, lifting him from the ground.

"I...told...you..." the elf squeaked. "If...you...force...me...to...help...you...with...the...curse...it...won't... work."

Haiden ignored the elf's words, continuing to pour power into the freezing enchantment as he dug with his free hand into every pocket in the elf's clothing, as well as yanking off more than one necklace. When he was satisfied that the creature carried no more talismans, he let his song drop away.

"I'm not here about my curse," he said shortly. "You're going to help me with something else entirely."

"I won't willingly help you with anything," the elf told him.

"Then I'll kill you," said Haiden blandly. Ember's comfortable belief that he wasn't a killer was far from his mind. "I know you're trying to kill Ember, and I'd rather kill you first and know that you're no further threat to her." He stared unblinkingly into the elf's emerald eyes, which were showing their first gleam of true fear. "Unless you can be of some use to me, of course."

"What do you want?" the elf spat.

"I want you to take me to her island," Haiden said promptly. "The one she comes from."

"How am I supposed to do that?" the elf demanded, not even attempting to deny knowledge of the island.

"I'm sure you have a way," said Haiden. "If you're behind the sacrifices to the so-called monster, which I don't doubt, then you have a way of contacting the Protector."

The elf's eyes widened, clearly caught off-guard by the specificity of Haiden's knowledge.

"What's it going to be?" Haiden demanded, tightening his fist to emphasize his point. The elf's hands scrabbled against his grip, and he let out another song, directing the magic to stay on the elf's form this time, and freeze him in place. "Will you take me to the island, or do I kill you now?"

The elf's eyes bulged from the pressure of Haiden's fist, and he had to remind himself to lift the enchantment enough to allow his captive to speak.

"I'll...take...you," the elf rasped. "I have...a...boat."

Haiden nodded, the motion bringing into view the confiscated talismans littering the floor. He frowned as one caught his eye. It wasn't unusual for talismans to be made of precious metals—especially gold—or even gemstones. But this one was an unfamiliar type of material.

Maintaining his grip on the elf, he stooped down and picked it up in his free hand. He turned it over, studying it in the torchlight. The stone had clearly been worked by a master hand. It was perfectly round, more so than any pearl, and its surface was a polished black. But the flickering light of the fires revealed threads of red and purple that seemed to dance before his eyes, setting it apart from any normal onyx or agate.

Regal onyx. It must be.

"This is from the island," he said slowly. "That's what

your interest is. What did you do, trade magical protection in exchange for this?" He turned it over in his hand. "I'm guessing it's an excellent conductor of magic?" He could think of no other reason why an elf would carry it around as a talisman, having first worked it into a perfect sphere. Circles were the most effective shape in storing and channeling magic.

He looked up to see the elf glowering at him, and he gave the little creature a shake. The burden of holding him was wearing away at Haiden's strength, but he didn't allow his arm to so much as wobble.

"Answer me!" he shouted into the elf's face. "Did you put up the magical barrier in exchange for regal onyx?"

"Yes," the elf spat, resentment written across his face.

"And the sacrificed maidens?" Haiden demanded. "Why was that necessary?"

"That wasn't my idea," the elf said. "That's the affair of the so-called Protector."

Anger flashed through Haiden. So-called indeed. Based on what Ember had told him of the island community, he could imagine why the leader had chosen such a barbaric way to meet the elf's demands. Fear and control went hand in hand.

He shook his head in disgust. It took a true monster to murder innocent girls under his power in order to solidify the impression that he was protecting the community from which they came.

"All I demanded was the payment of more regal onyx every five years," the elf went on. "I was to meet them at the halfway point in a boat, for delivery. I didn't know he was going to send the onyx sewed into the gowns of the girls until the first shipment was made."

"So what happened to the girls after you took the onyx

from their clothes?" Haiden demanded. The elf didn't immediately answer, and he shook him again. "Well?"

"I bear no responsibility for their fate," said the elf belligerently. "It wasn't my choice to send them out onto the ocean as carriers of the cargo. The whole bargain was based on the mutual agreement to keep the island's existence a secret. The Protector must have known the terms of the bargain would require me to dispose of them."

"Dispose of them?" Haiden repeated, disgusted. "I should kill you right now." But his words were empty. He was unlikely to reach the island and help Ember disillusion her people without the elf's involvement. "You don't deserve reprieve," he said. "You're a monster."

"Fine words, coming from you." The elf attempted to scoff, but with Haiden's fist still around his throat, the sound came out more like a squeak.

"I'm far from perfect, but I was never a monster like you are," said Haiden dismissively. "No matter what you or anyone saw when you looked at me."

*No matter what my mother saw,* added a silent voice in his head. And with the thought came an incredible sense of release. It was true, and perhaps for the first time in his life, he actually believed it. Of everyone who'd seen him, the good, the bad, the surface, what was underneath...it had been Ember who'd been right in her assessment of who he was. And instead of accepting her words, he'd pushed her away in anger.

He had to reach her in time.

Haiden pocketed the regal onyx and let out a quiet song, using magic to strengthen his arm and lessen the elf's weight. He wasn't about to trust the elf to freely guide them.

"Where's your boat?" he demanded.

Begrudgingly, the elf directed him, and it wasn't long

before Haiden was throwing his captive into a small but sturdy rowboat. It wasn't elf-made. It fit them both comfortably, with oars large enough for Haiden to wield. No doubt the elf had used magic to propel himself across the water on his infrequent voyages. This theory was borne out by the way the boat moved in the water. The whole thing seemed to be enhanced by magic, its passage too smooth and fast even for the propitious tide. Haiden began to feel a trickle of hope that they might actually catch up to Ember while still on the water.

The magic enhancement wasn't the only thing making the boat move, the little sails soon billowing nicely in the breeze. Knowing that his access to magic would be more limited on the water than on land, Haiden sang while he worked, drawing as much power into himself as he could hold.

Once they were far enough into the water for Haiden to be confident they were traveling the right way—so unerringly, he suspected the magic of assisting there, too— Haiden looked at the elf. The creature was huddled on the far side of the boat, his eyes on Haiden. No doubt he would take the first opportunity to do him an injury, or seize the regal onyx talisman back.

Haiden didn't intend to give him that chance. He released all his stored power in a song, coating the elf with a freezing enchantment. When his reserves were depleted, he turned his back on his unwilling companion, curling up in the bottom of the boat without a word. He would sleep while the magic was in place, and stay awake the rest of the voyage if necessary.

His sleep was far from restful, but he did manage a few hours. When he woke, the sky was already lightening beyond their bow. The elf looked furious, but remained frozen in the position where Haiden had left him. Haiden knew the creature deserved every discomfort, but he was too angry and disgusted even to feel smug. How many girls had this elf murdered the way he'd tried to murder Ember?

"So what was the bargain?" he asked, when the magic finally lifted, and the elf began to stir. "You kept the island secret, by means of creating a magical barrier and whatever else necessary, and this *Protector* gave you enough regal onyx to fund all your activities?"

The elf just glared at him, but Haiden had no doubt his assessment was accurate. He squinted toward the sun, now well above the horizon, and adjusted the sails slightly.

"But how did it all start?" Haiden mused. "I suppose the Protector found you when he came to Providore thirty years ago, after those fishermen sailed east and never returned."

Again, the elf said nothing.

"Ember must have been right about there being some kind of barrier in place before then. I suppose it was put there by her ancestors when they first reached the island. And it took generations to wear off, whereas yours has to be replenished every five years. A bit pathetic, really."

"Mine is far stronger than the old one," snapped the elf, predictably rising to the bait. "No one's been able to get past it."

"I came pretty close," said Haiden fairly. "And I'm about to pass it again."

The elf scoffed. "You won't. Neither of us will survive if you try to go through the barrier."

"I'm not too sure about that," said Haiden conversationally. "I remember from last time that it was very painful, but I'm not afraid of pain. I turned back then, but I won't now."

"Then you'll die," the elf said sharply. "What good does it do you to kill us both?"

"I don't think I will die," said Haiden. "Not if my theory is correct that the barrier is simply pure, wild magic. I'm a singer, so while it would be fatal to other humans, I don't think it will be to me."

The elf now wore a very arrested look, giving Haiden the impression that he hadn't thought of that possibility. It wasn't likely that any of the people who'd previously sailed close to the barrier had been singers—they weren't common, and in this remote corner of Vadolis, they were almost unheard of.

"Are you willing to risk your life on the chance that you're right?" the elf demanded.

"Absolutely," Haiden assured him. "And your life too, now you mention it."

The elf ground his teeth together angrily, his little eyes darting around the boat as if looking for a means of escape.

"Although," Haiden realized aloud, "I suppose you'll die regardless, won't you? You're not a singer. You can manipulate mined magic, but your body can't process it, can it? That's a shame."

"You don't need me here," the elf hissed. "You have the boat—if you're determined to continue to the island, you can do that without me."

Haiden gave an unpleasant laugh. "You're coming with me, my slippery little friend. You've been a silent menace to Ember's community for far too long. It's time to bring you out into the open, let them see what they've really been living in fear of."

The elf said nothing, but his panic was palpable. As the morning wore on, Haiden watched his agitation increase. He, on the other hand, felt perfectly at ease. He watched the elf squirm as he consumed the dried meat he'd found in the boat's storage compartment. Judging by the presence of emergency supplies, the vessel doubled as a means of escape in a crisis.

Haiden could tell when they drew close to the barrier, both from the elf's demeanor and from the magic radiating toward him. It grew in intensity, much like the sensation of increasing heat that came from walking steadily toward a large fire.

"Last chance," Haiden said pleasantly. "If you want to remove the barrier, you'd better do it quickly. Or we'll find out exactly how fatal it is or isn't to each of us."

"I can't," the elf snapped. "It's part of the bargain."

Haiden shrugged. "A despicable bargain, that I have no obligation to honor. That's not my problem."

"You'll die same as me!" the elf shrieked, as Haiden felt the first prickles of pain from the magic of the barrier.

But the claim lacked conviction, and Haiden didn't flinch. He was ready to face much more than some physical pain if it meant helping Ember. He could only hope that she'd survived the passage, if she was truly ahead of him.

"Last chance," he repeated, bracing his body as the pain increased.

The elf let out a scream of frustration, then his body slumped in defeat. "Destroy the onyx talisman," he spat out. "The barrier is tied to it."

The pain was strong enough now that Haiden didn't hesitate to obey. He pulled out the sphere, dropping it in the bottom of the boat. He saw the elf's beady eyes dart to it, but he didn't give his companion any time to act. Yanking his blade from his belt, he brought the hilt smashing down on the stone once, twice, three times. The sphere shattered under the impact, not coming apart completely, but fracturing in multiple places.

Haiden felt the magic of the barrier shudder and then

give way, and the next moment, the boat passed through clear, empty water. He could see a smudge up ahead—the first glimpse of Ember's island. They'd been quick, but not quick enough to catch Ember before she made landfall. He could only hope that she'd survived the barrier, and that they'd be in time to help her if she ran into trouble once she reached the island.

And knowing Ember, he thought ruefully, trouble would find her immediately.

# CHAPTER SEVENTEEN

# Ember

Ember's little boat shuddered as the prow hit the rocks.

She was back.

She clambered gratefully from the vessel, grimacing at the splintered section of wood that had just made contact with land. She'd been lucky to keep it afloat all the way to the island. The woeful state of it made her feel marginally less guilty about the fact that she'd stolen the vessel. But only marginally.

"If I make it out of this alive, I'll pay you back twice what the boat was worth," she promised the absent owner resolutely. "If not, then...well, I suppose I'll be remembered as a thief, and I'll just have to live with that."

Or rather, not live with it, but this was all beside the point.

Ember secured the boat clumsily to an outcropping of rock, although it hardly seemed worth it. She took a moment to steel herself, then began to climb up the jagged section of cliff. She'd known better than to sail up to the wharf. She needed to make her presence known in as public a location as possible. If the Protector got wind of her return before she'd been widely seen, she'd be quietly eliminated for certain.

And she hadn't gone through such pain and effort to get here only to be silenced before she told her tale to a single person.

Pain was the word. She shuddered at the memory of the agony that had gripped her when she reached the invisible barrier. What had felt like a steady, cleansing flow of rain on her voyage away from the island had felt more like being doused in boiling wax on her way toward it. Her feeble attempts to protect herself with song had yielded very little effect, and it had taken everything in her to keep directing her boat forward and not turn back. She wasn't at all surprised that Haiden had turned his vessel around when he'd first encountered the barrier five years ago. She would have done the same had the stakes of her mission not been so high.

Her persistence had been rewarded, though, and Haiden's speculation proven correct. The magic was painful —excruciatingly so—but not fatal. Once she passed through it, the pain had receded, and she could find no lingering sign of ill-effect.

She had, in fact, reached the island with her full strength. She crested the cliff and, after peering cautiously around to ensure no one was in sight, she crept forward. The ground beneath her feet felt alive in a way it never had before. How had she lived all her life here without ever feeling the power that emanated in a constant, gentle flow from the island itself? Now that she'd discovered her singing ability, and Haiden had taught her to unlock her extra sense, the presence of the magic practically screamed in her mind with every step.

The thought bolstered her, filling her with hope that she truly was going to have the strength to face down the Protector and his lies. Ember moved into a nearby copse, trying to get her bearings. Where exactly had she landed? The sound of hooves made her pause, and she peered out from behind a tree. She'd emerged near a road, and a farm horse was plodding slowly toward her, pulling a weathered cart. A man was riding up on the cart, and a young boy was walking alongside, steadying the tottering load of hay with an upraised plank of wood.

Following the road with her eyes, Ember thought she recognized her location. She was on the southern edge of the island, nowhere near her home, but not far from the main town.

Impulsively, she stepped out in front of the cart.

"Excuse me," she said pleasantly. "Do you think you could give me a ride to market?"

The man pulled his horse up with a *whoa*, his eyes widening as they passed over her.

"Ember?"

She winced. She hadn't remembered his name, only vaguely recognizing him as a farmer, and had therefore hoped he wouldn't know her. But she should have realized that being chosen as a sacrifice would ensure she was universally known.

"Yes, it's me," she said. "I'm back."

"But...you were eaten by the monster," the farmer said stupidly. The boy stood alongside the cart still, staring at her with his mouth hanging open.

"Actually, the monster doesn't eat people," said Ember impatiently. She closed her eyes in irritation with herself. "No, that's not what I meant to say. There is no monster. At least, not like we thought. It's actually—"

She cut herself off as she opened her eyes, seeing the blank incomprehension on the man's face. She was certainly making a mess of this.

"Can you take me to market?"

"Not sure I should," the farmer said nervously. "It's all very irregular."

Ember restrained her impatience. How quickly she'd forgotten the rigid control under which the island's inhabitants conducted every aspect of their lives.

"Listen," she said desperately. "Everything we've been told is a lie. Our borders aren't protected by a monster, and there was never any need to sacrifice people. It's all a lie to control us. Singers aren't killers, or evil, and the magic the Protector uses to claim his right to rule is nothing more than a trick."

The man's eyes were bulging out of his head now, but she had a sinking feeling it was more in horror at finding himself in conversation with a madwoman—or perhaps a ghost—than in betrayal at discovering he'd been lied to.

"This needs to be reported," he said, his eyes on her but his words more for himself. He slapped the horse's rump with the reins, urging the animal back into motion.

"No, wait!" Ember said, but it was futile.

The man had picked up the pace, glancing behind him with mingled fear and relief, as though he'd just escaped a dangerous threat. Ember fought down panic. He was surely going to tell the Protector's people, and she'd be hunted down swiftly. She looked about her, trying to formulate a plan, and realized with a start that the young boy was still standing there, watching her with mouth agape.

"It's all right," she told him, his stupefied expression sending a trickle of amusement through her in spite of the situation. "I won't hurt you. And I am telling the truth," she added for good measure.

The boy didn't move, didn't so much as blink.

"Is it a market day?" Ember asked briskly. She'd lost track of what day it was.

Confronted with an easy topic, the boy nodded earnestly, his mouth closing in the process. "Always is, day after rest day."

It was good news for her plans, but Ember couldn't help a surge of nerves. "Do you know who my parents are?"

Again he nodded. "Everyone does. People avoid 'em now. They're marked, ya know?"

Ember winced. "I know. Will you find them for me? Tell them I'm back and I need to see them urgently? Tell them I'm going to the market square."

He stared, his eyes wider than ever, but after a painful moment he gave yet another nod.

"Thanks," said Ember breathlessly. Turning away, she took off, jogging in the direction the cart had gone. She would have to be quick if she was to reach town before the Protector sent someone looking for her in response to the farmer's report.

But the first dwellings of the main town were still out of reach when a lone figure appeared on the path ahead. At first Ember increased her pace, thinking she'd found another opportunity to tell her tale, but as the man's form came properly into view, she pulled up with a gasp.

The Protector's brother. He looked more tense than she'd ever seen him, and the moment he recognized her, she saw his features transform.

"It is you," he hissed, enraged.

"Yes, I'm back." Ember planted her feet, deciding it was best to face him head on. If only she'd had the chance to learn the trick Haiden had mentioned, of drawing magic into her body and holding it temporarily until ready to use it. But she hadn't, so she waited. "I feel very important," she told him conversationally. "That you came yourself, instead of sending an underling."

"How?" the leader growled, ignoring her remark. "How did you get back here?"

"Magic," Ember said flippantly.

For the briefest of moments, she and her adversary just stared at each other. Then he lunged, the movement so swift, Ember barely had time to dodge. She caught the flash of silver as she leaped out of the way. He wasn't messing around. He might prefer to get answers from her first about how she'd gotten back through the barrier, but he wouldn't wait for them if it would risk her surviving to tell her story.

Ember's heart beat frantically as she leaped away from him, but her determination was greater than her fear. She had no weapon, same as the last time this man had tried to kill her, but this time she wasn't defenseless.

She raised her voice in a furious song, urging the magic up from the ground and into herself.

"*Blow him away!*" She practically screamed the song, not having the skill to attempt anything complicated.

The power swirled out from her, turning into a roaring wind with impressive speed. The air burst on the Protector's brother, sending his arms flinging wide so that the blade went flying. Ember kept singing, encouraging the wind onward. The Protector's brother put his arms over his face, shouting in anger as he was buffeted backward. His protests only made Ember redouble her efforts. With another almighty cry, she sent a new gust of wind upward, and watched with satisfaction as the Protector's brother was swept up into the air and sent flying into the upper branches of a tree on the edge of the path.

Ember stayed only to ensure that he was stuck in the tree. He was too high to jump down safely—he'd have to climb, if he could extricate himself from the branches.

She turned her back on him, sprinting toward the town as fast as she could go. Urgency drove her on, past the point where her lungs demanded she stop. To her elation, she soon saw the first buildings, and not long after, heard the bustle of the market. She was almost there.

She was passing other inhabitants now, but she didn't speak to any of them. It was imperative that she gained as big an audience as possible before any of the leaders caught up to her. She burst into the market square, panting as she pushed her way through the throng. A few people let out gasps as they recognized her, but most didn't get a good enough look as she barreled past them. The crowd was already buzzing with the unmistakable hum of gossip. The farmer must have spread his tale further than just the Protector.

So much the better.

But when Ember reached the dais where the Protector had stood the day he announced her fate, she saw that many of the market-goers weren't looking at her. They were still locked in excited conversations.

"Listen!" she cried. "Everyone listen to me!"

Those closest to the dais turned at her shout, and gradually, the crowd took notice. The cries of shock, and the astonishment on the faces upturned to hers made Ember question whether the gossip had really been about her return, or about something else. But there was no time to waste on speculation.

"Everyone!" she called again. "Listen, this is important!"

Her eyes picked out Noani, watching in open-mouthed astonishment. She wished her parents could hear her as well, but if Noani was there, it wasn't their market day. And they would never deviate from the routine set before them.

"You all thought I was dead, I'm sure," she said, her voice carrying clearly into the sudden hush. "But I'm very much alive. I've been to the mainland, and it's nothing like we were told! We've been lied to all our lives. There's no reason we need to be concealed from the mainland. The people there don't hate us, or want to kill us!"

"She escaped the monster," someone called out, aghast. "She broke faith, and that's why the protections have lifted. That's why boats are coming for us from the mainland!"

Murmurs and cries passed through the crowd, and at the mention of boats, Ember thought she understood. Someone must have seen her vessel approaching, and spread the word that the protections were gone. That must be what everyone had been talking about before she arrived.

"I'm not the one who's broken faith!" she said, her voice clear and confident. "The Protector did, when he lied to us!"

To her frustration, she saw many faces darken at this disparagement of the revered leader.

"The monster will come for us all," someone moaned.

"There's no monster!" she insisted. "It was all a lie!"

Her words were met, not with relief, but with shrill screams of terror. It took Ember a moment to realize that the crowd's attention was no longer on her. Everyone's eyes had flicked to the edge of the market square.

Frowning, Ember squinted over the crowd. Her heart seemed to stop in her chest at the sight of a familiar, over-sized figure, his grotesque boar features looming over everyone else's heads. With one hand, he half-dragged the elf from the wharf by the arm.

Ember's heart started back at double time, warmth rushing through her. Haiden had come for her? Was it *his* boat, then, that had been seen by the lookouts?

"No monster?!" someone screamed shrilly. "She's in league with the creature, and led it here to slaughter us!"

Pandemonium broke out, people starting to flee in all directions. Ember's delight at seeing Haiden gave way to the irritated realization that his timing was actually incredibly unfortunate. No one would take her story seriously now.

"No, there is a monster!" she called desperately over the chaos. "But not like we thought. He's right there." She gestured to the newcomers, her gaze following her arm.

Haiden had stopped halfway across the market square, his stormy eyes fixed on her with a long-suffering expression that seemed to say, *seriously*?

Ember was seized by an absurd, near-hysterical urge to laugh.

"I was talking about the elf," she called to him, with an apologetic shrug. It wasn't like anyone else was listening to her anyway.

Haiden strode the rest of the way over, still dragging the elf behind him. "Subtlety is wasted on these people," he informed her. "Monstrous features mean monster, that's as deep as you can expect."

Ember was about to protest in defense of her people, but the anxiety in his eyes stopped her as he scanned her figure.

"Are you all right?"

She nodded. "I'm fine."

"You shouldn't have run away like that," he scolded her, his eyes at their stormiest. "You scared me."

She raised an eyebrow. "I thought you said you weren't afraid."

"I lied," he responded shortly.

The warmth was back in Ember's chest, but a quick glance at the melee around them reminded her that it wasn't the time for a private chat.

"I need them to listen," she said desperately. "This is probably my only chance to convince them."

Haiden gave a curt nod, drawing himself up to his full, illusory height. He opened his mouth and let out a roar that Ember realized, from the stirring in her senses, was half song. Power swirled up and into him before pouring out over the crowd.

They stilled, whether from magic or from fear of the beast's rage, Ember couldn't tell.

"Next one to move gets eaten," Haiden bellowed.

That brought instant stillness to the crowd, all of whom had been raised to respond to demands for absolute obedience. But Ember gave Haiden an unimpressed look.

"That's not going to help me convince them that they're not in danger from any monster."

He just grunted. "Say your piece."

But Ember didn't get the chance to say more. In spite of the crowd's attempts to stay motionless, a ripple was passing through it. Squinting through the mass of people, Ember recognized who was approaching. Fear clutched at her heart, and she grabbed Haiden's arm.

"That's the Protector."

He followed her gaze, his absurd features hardening.

"Protector!" someone shrieked in evident relief. "The monster has come for us. Pacify him, like you did last time!"

The grizzled man emerged at the front of the crowd, and Ember saw him freeze as he caught sight of the trio on the dais. For a moment, she had the satisfaction of seeing panic flash through his eyes. Whatever he'd expected, it hadn't been to find an actual, real-life monster on his island. He knew perfectly well that the creature before him was not the monster he'd deceitfully described to his people. And he must know that appealing to the creature in accordance with the tale he'd spun for the community would yield nothing but confusion from the unknown boar-man. He couldn't even order that the "monster" be killed summarily, because he'd conditioned his people to believe the creature was all that was keeping them safe from the terrible threat of the mainland.

It was immensely satisfying to have the upper hand on him, even if only for a moment.

"Well?" she asked, her expression cold. "Aren't you going to treat with the monster? Shouldn't he recognize you from your previous encounter?"

"I've never seen him before in my life," said Haiden coldly.

A ripple of unease passed through the crowd. So far they were confused more than suspicious, but Ember felt a bubble of hope. The Protector's lies were starting to be exposed.

"Ember," said the Protector, clearly thinking fast. "Your return to us is...miraculous."

"Yes," Ember agreed pleasantly. "The most miraculous part was that I managed to survive when your brother attempted to murder me the moment we rowed far enough from the island."

A couple of shocked cries, quickly stifled, rang out from those closest to the dais. And one cry from further back. Ember's eyes flicked up, her breath catching at the sight of her parents entering the market square, their faces awash with emotion as they stared up at her. But she couldn't afford to get distracted by their presence yet. She looked back in front of her to catch the murderous look on the Protector's face before he schooled his features.

"Ember, what has overtaken you?" he asked mournfully. "I can't imagine what you hope to gain from such lies, but—"

"There he is." Ember cut him off, pointing an accusing finger at the man who'd just appeared at the back of the crowd. "He tried to kill me not half an hour ago, as well. To stop me reaching the market and telling you all the truth."

"My poor child, I tried merely to restrain you for your own good," the Protector's brother called out. "The tainted magic of the mainland has addled your mind."

"I fear you are right, brother," the Protector said, his voice laden with sadness. He turned to his entourage. "Restrain her, but be gentle."

Ember tensed, but before anyone could move, Haiden stepped in front of her.

"If anyone touches her," he growled, "I really will start killing people."

"Wait!"

A woman pushed forward from the throng, and with a lurch of the heart, Ember recognized her. She was the mother of Diana, the "sacrifice" prior to Ember.

"So what happened to the others?" she demanded. "If they weren't sacrificed to this monster, where are they?"

"I don't know," Ember said, miserably aware that she'd failed in her vow to learn the fate of the other girls. "But Haiden never saw them." Seeing the woman's confusion, she signaled to Haiden, adding, "Him. The supposed monster."

"I know what happened to them, though." Haiden's

voice was grim. "Your so-called Protector used them as vessels. He put them in a boat and sent them toward the mainland, with regal onyx sewn into their clothes in payment to this miserable monster."

On the last word, he lifted the elf before him, so the creature's feet left the ground. Curiously, the elf didn't resist. He seemed much weaker than on the other occasion Ember had seen him. Gasps and murmurs passed through the crowd. Of course no one on the island had seen an elf before.

"And once he'd taken the payment," Haiden went on, dropping a large and fractured chunk of regal onyx onto the ground before him, "the elf killed them."

Diana's mother let out a cry that was gut-wrenching to hear. Ember felt bile rise up in her throat, and forced it down. Haiden's eyes—the only human part of his face— were narrowed in disgust as he looked down at the elf. Abruptly, he let go of him, as though unable to stand touching the creature any longer. The elf fell, not catching his footing in time to avoid crumpling to the ground.

"These are all lies."

The Protector strode up onto the dais, brushing past Haiden. Ember saw his eyes flick to the elf then quickly away. So he recognized one of the pair. The Protector raised his arms appealingly to the crowd, and to her frustration, Ember saw many eyes turned to him in relieved desperation, as if sure he would make sense of it all for them.

"My dear friends, we have all been betrayed and deceived, but rest assured, I will not let this disaster endanger you all. Whatever failure of the barrier allowed these trespassers through will be investigated, and whoever is responsible will be brought to justice for—"

"It wasn't my fault!"

The shrill voice of the elf cut across the Protector, and the creature staggered to his feet. Ember couldn't imagine what Haiden had done to him, but the elf was clearly in a bad way. She could see no physical injuries, but he was panting heavily, clutching at his chest as if it was difficult to draw breath. His eyes fixed on the Protector, their expression conveying both anger and desperation.

"It wasn't my fault I had to remove the barrier." He gestured furiously at Haiden. "He forced me! You have to do something, or the magic of our bargain will kill me."

# CHAPTER EIGHTEEN

# Ember

"I have no idea what you're talking about," the Protector protested, his face pale. "I've never seen you before."

"I won't die for your secrets!" The elf's voice was more shrill than ever. "I've done my part for thirty years to keep your island concealed, as we agreed. The biggest ever threat to your discovery is her." He pointed dramatically at Ember, who glowered back. "And I tried to eliminate her, like I eliminated the others for you. But this worm got in the way at every turn."

"It's almost like it wasn't worth your while to make an enemy of me out of pure spite," Haiden growled.

Ember was less interested in their confrontation than in the reaction of the crowd. The elf's claims had rattled many onlookers. Their expressions were doubtful as they looked between the Protector and the astonishing collection of visitors. Was it possible this would work? Would the community finally see the truth?

"Do you think I'm afraid of you as an enemy?" the elf spat. "It's her arrival that ruined everything." Ember looked around to find him watching her with a mad gleam in his eyes. "She's the real threat to the secret I vowed to keep. If I silence her, surely the magic will be satisfied."

Before Ember understood his intention, he lunged toward her, his hands outstretched.

She heard Haiden's cry, but he'd clearly been taken by surprise as well, because neither he nor Ember had mustered a song when something flew through the air with a whistling sound, and the elf dropped to the ground in front of Ember. She stared at him for several bewildered seconds before she could make sense of what had happened. His eyes were closed, his face more ashen than ever, and his form completely still. Her eyes passed from the wound on his head, to the rock on the ground beside him, and up to see Diana's mother still standing right at the front of the crowd. Her wide eyes were fixed on the elf's unmoving form, and her chest was heaving.

After a moment of stunned silence, her gaze moved to Ember's face.

"He killed my daughter," she whispered, the hoarse words carrying through the hush. "I couldn't let him kill you too."

"Thank you," Ember told her, her throat thick. She looked again at the elf, then at Haiden. "Is he dead?"

"I think so," he said quietly. "I don't think the rock would have killed him on its own. He's been expiring slowly since he lifted the barrier to save his own life. He broke the old bargain and activated the magic attached to it. I think this end was inevitable."

"She killed it." The murmur passed through the crowd.

"Does that mean she's a singer? Or not, because it wasn't human?" someone asked, confused.

"Singing has nothing to do with killing," Ember started, but she got no further.

At a gesture from the Protector, several of his assistants surged up onto the dais toward her. Haiden leaped over the elf's still form, intercepting one with a roar. He sent the man flying with his fist, a song building as he turned to the next one.

"Seize them both!" the Protector cried.

The nearest man hesitated, clearly reluctant to take on the boar-man. And Ember could see the confusion in the crowd as the Protector ordered the arrest of the monster who'd supposedly kept them all safe for three decades.

But many others were still ready to do their leader's bidding. Others from the crowd surged forward, and Ember seized Haiden's arm.

"Don't hurt them," she pleaded. "None of them understand."

His eyes met hers, and she could read the conflict in their depths. He didn't want to attack the victims of the Protector's lies any more than she did. But his determination to protect her was evident, and it made her heart feel like it was singing, even while her voice was silent.

The distraction was enough to allow two men to seize Ember by the arms. She saw the Protector gesturing for them to remove her from the dais, but she had no intention of going meekly.

"No!" she shouted at the leader, struggling against the men. She tried to make her voice as loud as possible, hoping everyone would hear. "I won't let you drag me away somewhere. Whatever you plan to do to me, you can do it in front of everyone."

The Protector's face remained impassive. No doubt he

thought her powerless and didn't doubt his ability to contain her. But he didn't know how much she'd changed since she left the island.

Out of the corner of her eye she saw the tall form of the Protector's brother fighting his way through the crowd, and heard him shout to his brother to gag her. But it was too late.

She opened her mouth and released a song with all the force she had in her. Magic poured from the ground into her body. It was more than responsive—it was eager. The magic of the island had barely been accessed for generations. It swelled beneath her feet, potent and clamoring to be free.

She didn't even summon wind this time. She just released the magic in a torrent, and the men holding her were thrown backward as if struck with a physical blow. She turned to see the Protector's eyes wide with horror. In the moment before he acted, she read on his face that this was the one truth he'd most desired to hide—the reality of what singing was. That was why he'd gone against the routines he'd established, claiming that the monster demanded a new sacrifice as soon as his brother discovered her singing ability. She couldn't be allowed to live and possibly learn to harness songcraft.

If everyone learned what singing and magic really were, the whole foundation of lies on which he'd built the island's history and culture would crumble.

Ember saw the Protector's desperation, but she didn't turn her magic on him. He wouldn't act against her in front of so many witnesses. But either she underestimated his desperation, or he overestimated the absolute hold he had over his people. Because before her would-be captors had picked themselves up, the Protector moved forward into the space they'd occupied.

His movements were subtle—Ember barely caught the flash of silver as he produced a blade from somewhere. She hadn't even raised her hands in defense, but someone else had seen much more clearly than she had.

"NO!"

Haiden's roar was too melodic for normal speech, and before Ember's eyes, a sword flew from the hand of one of the Protector's felled guards and sped toward the leader. The Protector didn't seem to see it, but Haiden's shout propelled him into action nevertheless. Ember watched, transfixed, as he lunged toward her, only to slam to a halt as the magic-guided sword sailed unerringly past her and straight into his chest.

For a moment their eyes locked, the older man's unnervingly devoid of emotion. Ember felt numb herself as he crumpled to the floor like a rag doll. It took her a moment to realize she was swaying, and to comprehend the white-hot pain that was rapidly driving back her numbness.

She looked slowly down at her body, unable to make sense of the sight of the Protector's blade still protruding from her stomach. She blinked, her vision blurring as red pooled around the wound, barely comprehending that the horrible, gurgling choke she could hear was coming from her own lips.

This was how she died. After everything she'd been through to be free of this man and his control, he—whom she'd never known to do his own dirty work—had been the one to deal the killing blow.

Ember heard the screams of the crowd, but they meant nothing to her. Only one voice broke through the fog as her body finally gave way.

A voice that exploded with a passion that put the falseness of the island's leader to shame, even in death.

"EMBER!"

She couldn't see Haiden—she couldn't see much of anything—but she felt his arms around her as he caught her. They were strong, human arms, and even through the pain now spreading into every inch of her body, she knew their touch, and felt safe inside their circle.

And she felt the explosion of magic that went out from his cry. Her mind couldn't make sense of much, but everyone in the vicinity seemed to be flat on the ground. Everyone except Haiden, who knelt on the dais, his voice broken, and his monstrous features twisted in agony as he held her.

"Ember!" he cried. "Ember, stay with me! Ember, you can't die!"

"Haiden," she whispered. "Did they see? Do they know who killed me?"

"I...I don't know...I think so," he said desperately.

She nodded, satisfied. A rasping cough escaped her before she managed to speak again. "Then there's hope that they'll...be free of...the lies."

"Ember, don't you dare tell yourself you can die in peace now!" Haiden raged. He seemed to be trying to stem the flow of blood from her middle, but she could feel her life draining away from her. "I refuse to give you peace!" Haiden was babbling on. "I won't let you give up!"

She felt something hot drop on her face, and realized he was crying over her.

"I never mastered healing magic," Haiden said brokenly. "I never could find the gentleness it requires." Ember's eyes were closed now, but she heard him catch his breath. "But I understand core magic! Core magic is strong enough to do things nothing else can achieve."

Ember frowned. She'd read his notes—core magic was as dangerous as he'd said. But she was too weak to say so. Too weak to say anything, to move, even to open her eyes.

Haiden started to sing, the melody low and ferocious. Ember felt magic stirring beneath them then wrapping around her. It was comforting and warm, but she didn't think it was making a difference. She was fairly certain it was too late for that.

"I can't do it," Haiden cried, his anguished words cutting off his own song. "I'm not strong enough to do it alone. It's the deepest kind of heart magic, and this land won't give me its heart."

"It's...all...right," Ember whispered, the words escaping her as little more than a breath.

"No, it's not!" he cried. His arms tightened around her. "Help me, Ember. Please, I'm begging you, help me! I'll bring the skill, I'll mold the magic. But help me find the heart magic. It will respond to you."

Ember forced her eyes open with an effort, her hand shaking as it found his face, somewhere in the region of his illusory neck.

"I...can't."

"Yes, you can!" Haiden said fiercely. "Please, you have to help me. I can't bear for you to die. I can't live without you."

Ember's body was telling her she had nothing left to give, but her heart was incapable of resisting his plea. Swallowing, she forced her voice to respond, pushing out the most feeble song imaginable. Haiden's voice instantly joined hers, and she let the strength of his song carry her own weak melody. She focused instead on the ground beneath them, the island she knew so well. She called the magic into herself, imagining it wrapping around her very heart.

She'd read every one of Haiden's notes on core magic, and although they'd been technical and confusing, she'd understood enough to give direction to her efforts. She urged the magic she could feel around her heart to take hold of her essence, giving it permission to draw on every last ounce of her fading energy to power the enchantment she wanted to give to Haiden. It was a last act she didn't begrudge for a moment.

And yet, incredibly, impossibly, as she poured the magic from her very core into his, she felt her energy strengthen. Something invisible coated itself around her heart, bracing it where it was weak, giving it new strength.

And all the while, Haiden's voice was rising, his melody getting surer and stronger as he sang words of healing. The numbness began to recede, Ember's mind clearing enough to register the pain that was taking its place. But even that pain faded in turn, as if it was a poison being drawn outward from the place where the Protector's knife had pierced her.

Still singing, she raised eyes that were no longer blurred to Haiden's face. Her amazement turned to pure wonder as she realized that it was his own face she saw. Gone were the twisted features of the boar-man. A very human Haiden held her in his arms, his eyes wet and his voice still wrapping around hers in a duet that felt more intimate than any embrace.

Ember let her voice die away, one hand feeling at her wound, and the other reaching for Haiden's face. His features were smooth and solid, the warmth of his skin under her fingers so distracting that she forgot to even be amazed that her injury was gone.

"Haiden," she whispered.

His song petered out as well, his eyes searching hers frantically. "Are you all right?"

Ember nodded, her chest almost too tight to draw breath. "It doesn't hurt anymore. You healed it, Haiden."

"I think we healed it together," he said, drawing her more tightly against him. "I could feel the magic of the land respond to you in a way it wouldn't to me."

"I felt it, too. It was like it wrapped around my heart, and let me draw something out of my heart to send into you. Is that...is that core magic?"

Haiden looked suddenly anxious again. "It certainly sounds like it. Ember, I didn't mean for you to do that. I just meant for you to draw on the magic of the land for me. Can you still feel a connection of power between you and me?"

Ember frowned as she took stock. "I think I can," she said, amazed.

Haiden groaned quietly. "Then you did use core magic, which means it will continue to drain your energy until it finishes you. I'll fix this, Ember, I swear it. I won't let it kill you."

"No, Haiden." Ember shook her head. "I feel the connection, but it's not draining me. I have more energy than I've ever had. I didn't just feel it going out from me—I felt something coming in." She touched her fingers tentatively to his chest, above his heart. "Coming in from you." Her eyes found his. "Did you use core magic on me as well?"

"It was the only magic I had any hope of accessing that might be strong enough to heal such a deadly wound," he told her. "But I promise, I don't begrudge it."

She smiled at him, her heart full from more than just the foreign yet familiar magic that was still encasing it.

"You're very handsome," she told him irrelevantly.

Haiden gave a splutter of laughter that wasn't at all steady. "Not like this I'm not," he said, then frowned. "Wait, you're looking at my face. Did I miss you casting an enchantment to counteract the illusion?"

She shook her head. "I think the curse is lifted," she told him. "I didn't do anything—your features just came into focus." She glanced sideways at the crowd, all of whom had picked themselves up now, and most of whom were staring at them. "Look—they're more bewildered than terrified now."

Haiden followed her gaze.

"But...how?"

Ember shrugged. "No idea. Was it because the elf who cursed you died?"

"I don't think so," said Haiden slowly. He brought his gaze back to her, and something clicked in place behind his eyes. "It was you," he said. "Or rather, me turning to you." He gave an incredulous laugh. "The elf said that in order to break the curse, I'd have to ask someone else for help, and that person would have to be both capable of helping me and willing to do it. But I vowed never to ask—I was too stubborn, and determined that I could break it alone. When I begged you to help me just now, I didn't mean to ask for your help to break my curse, and I doubt that's the scenario the elf had in mind when he crafted it. But it might just have been the first time in my life that I've admitted I wasn't strong enough on my own, and I not only desperately needed but desperately wanted someone to help me with something I couldn't live without. I suppose it was enough to satisfy the magic."

Ember smiled contentedly up at him.

"Well," she said. "It's no surprise how the curse made you look given the problem all along was apparently your own pigheadedness. But I'm delighted to be the one to help you overcome your boorish ways."

Haiden let out a laugh that was half-groan at her attempt at humor, but he didn't get a chance to respond further. Ember pushed herself up, cutting off the sound by pressing her lips to his.

Haiden froze for a moment, taken by surprise. Then his arms closed all the way around her, and he pulled her flush against him with enough force to elicit an involuntary gasp.

The next moment his lips claimed hers again, and Ember surrendered herself to the sensation of nearness. Her hands were pressed against his chest, and she felt completely safe and at home in his arms. One of his hands found its way up her back to tangle in her fiery curls, cradling her head and pulling her even closer. She freed her own hand to creep to his jaw, her fingers trailing over her own rough shaving work as her lips moved against his.

"Ember!"

The cry broke into the moment too soon for Ember's liking, but she pulled instantly back from Haiden nonetheless. Turning, she saw both of her parents clambering onto the dais, and disentangled herself from Haiden to embrace them.

"You're alive," her mother sobbed, as her father patted her awkwardly on the back. "We didn't...we never thought... I hardly—"

"It's all right, Mother," said Ember. "There's so much to say and so much to explain, but there'll be time enough for that."

She cast her eyes over the crowd and drew in a sharp

breath as she caught sight of a tall figure moving surreptitiously through the very back of the crowd. He must have lingered to see the outcome of the attack against her, but that had been a mistake. The moment she and Haiden had just shared hadn't been long enough for him to make a clean escape.

"Haiden! That's the Protector's brother, the one who first tried to kill me."

Haiden was already singing, drawing magic from the ground and flinging it toward the escaping henchman. Ember felt a curious sensation as he did so, like something flaring softly to life around her heart. But she didn't think too hard about it. There would be time later to explore whatever was going on with the core magic.

The Protector's brother broke into a run, but as Ember watched, he seemed to sprint straight into an invisible wall. He crumpled, and a few men leaped forward from the crowd to seize him. Apparently at least some of the island's inhabitants had seen enough to become suspicious of their leaders, and perhaps recognizing the turning of the tide, none of the Protector's usual assistants rushed to his defense. With a jolt, Ember realized that one of the men hauling the Protector's brother to his feet was Gil.

Good for him.

She brought her eyes back to her parents, and saw her father looking askance at Haiden.

"This is Haiden, Father, Mother," she said brightly. "I think you'll like him, once you get to know him."

"But...he was..." Her father floundered for a moment then, when she didn't come to his rescue, pushed on. "He was the monster."

Ember shook her head, smiling fondly up at Haiden. "He was never a monster. He just looked like one." She leaned her head against his shoulder. "And although he's a bit of a grumpy hermit, I'm sure he'll find a way to embrace family for my sake."

Her parents didn't look convinced by this description, but it was Haiden who spoke.

"I certainly will, and for my own sake as well as yours. I've been unforgivably selfish in disappearing on my sister for five years, and I really need to make it right."

"I'd love to meet her!" Ember said, turning to face him.

"Yes." Haiden looked hesitant, and she raised an eyebrow.

"Won't I like her?" A more alarming thought seized her, and she added, "Won't she like me?"

"She's wonderful," Haiden hastened to assure her. "And I have no doubt you'll both love each other. It's just, she comes with a bit of...fuss."

"What do you mean?" Ember asked warily.

He grimaced. "She's sort of the crown princess of the kingdom of Teren."

"What?" Ember squealed. "I thought you said you *weren't* secretly some kind of prince."

"I'm not," Haiden said, sounding affronted at the idea. "She and I are forest peasants. She just happened to marry the heir to the throne of a kingdom."

"Well." Ember blinked. "It's a lot to match."

"You don't have to match anything," Haiden said with a smile. "I much prefer the life of a grumpy hermit over life in a castle."

She grinned up at him. "I hate to tell you this, Haiden, but your days of being a grumpy hermit are over." She tilted her head to the side. "Well, I suppose you might still be grumpy. But you'll have me intruding unbearably into your solitude and making your life miserably cheerful."

"A terrible trial," Haiden assured her. "But I'm used to living with curses by now. I'll do my best to endure it."

And, apparently heedless of her parents standing nearby, and the bewildered, milling crowd, he lowered his lips to hers once more.

# Haiden

Haiden drew in a deep breath, enjoying the gentle breeze that stirred the outdoor walkway down which he was strolling. The exterior passageways were a favorite feature of the castle in Terenford.

"Perfect day to be outside," commented his companion.

Haiden smiled in agreement at his sister, his expression softening further as his gaze took in the infant settled on her hip. He'd been back in Terenford for two weeks, and he still wasn't used to the sight of Gisela with a baby in her arms. The discovery that he had a three-year-old niece and a baby nephew wasn't exactly astonishing, but it was an adjustment.

"I'm glad you didn't name him Haiden for your missing brother, or anything foolishly sentimental like that," he commented, ruffling the infant's head of curly black hair.

Gisela gave him a look. "Otto actually suggested it. But frankly, I was still too mad at you to consider it."

Haiden winced. "That's deserved," he said. "I really am sorry, Gisela. It was appalling of me to sneak off like that and never send word. It must have been awful thinking I might be dead."

"It was awful some days," she acknowledged. "But I never really believed you were dead. I could just tell somehow." She narrowed her eyes at him. "I've forgiven you for disappearing. I'm not sure I can forgive you for eloping rather than letting me be at your wedding." She looked down the path ahead of them. "Speaking of which…"

Haiden looked up, his heart lifting at the sight of his wife coming toward him.

Wife. He wasn't used to that, either, but he liked it immensely. The magic that still bound him and Ember together responded to her proximity as well, releasing a silent song of its own as she joined them.

"Ember," he said. "There you are."

"I was told to look for you both out here," Ember said, smiling cheerfully at Gisela. "But if I'm interrupting a sibling moment, I don't in the least mind coming back later."

"Not at all," said Gisela kindly. She'd taken an instant liking to Ember, as Haiden had hoped she would. "I was just scolding him, so it's the sort of sibling moment he'd probably like to be rescued from."

"What's he done now?" Ember asked, directing a pained look at Haiden.

"Eloped with you instead of enduring the pomp and ceremony that would have been inflicted on us as relatives of Her Highness over here if we'd showed up not yet married."

Gisela punched his arm lightly in protest, as Ember sent her an apologetic smile.

"I'm afraid that's my fault. I was the one who wanted a quiet, intimate ceremony on my island."

"No one's at fault," said Gisela reassuringly. "I was just teasing Haiden." She sighed. "And he's not wrong. The formalities can be a bit overwhelming." She smiled knowingly between the two of them. "But we put up with a great deal for love, don't we?"

"We certainly do," said Ember solemnly, although her eyes danced with mischief. "Some of us more than others."

"Oi," said Haiden, without heat.

"How did the appointment at the Academy of Song go, by the way?" Gisela asked suddenly.

Haiden gave a slow nod. "It was interesting. They agree that the core magic is still in place. There are ways we could look into removing it. We probably should one day. But Ember's not in a rush to do it, and…" He shrugged. "Neither am I."

His sister gave him another knowing smile. "You've changed," she informed him, adding quickly, "And I mean that in a good way. You've softened."

Haiden rolled his eyes at her, but her thoughts had already run ahead, anxiety touching her features.

"Are you sure it's safe to leave the core magic in place? I mean, it seemed like, last time, it was a parasite…one that could prove fatal."

"You can talk freely about it," Haiden assured her, recognizing her attempts to be delicate. "I'm finding everything that happened in our childhood much easier to talk about these days." He felt Ember slip her arm through his, and gladly pulled it tighter. "And they didn't think at the academy that the core magic would be a danger to Ember or me this time. They think it's because we both used core magic on each other, sort of mingling it in the same enchantment. Apparently it's like a constant exchange of energy between us. It's all a bit baffling—they said they've never encountered anything quite like it before—but it doesn't seem to be harming us."

"It's very romantic!" Ember said brightly.

"It is not romantic," said Haiden with a scoff.

She scowled at him. "It is!"

"Well..." He felt himself weakening as he looked down into her face, his own features stretching in a smile in spite of himself. "Maybe a little."

He tore his eyes away from Ember to see Gisela grinning at him. *Like I said,* her sisterly voice seemed to say smugly in his mind. *Softened.*

"Honestly," Gisela said aloud, "I can just hardly believe you actually managed to bring down a rising kingdom for a second time. Who would have thought that the elf princess's prophecy had a second meaning all these years!"

Haiden grunted. He was doubtful about Gisela's theory. "I don't think I'd call the island community a kingdom."

"I think it could be argued," said Ember fairly. "The Protector acted with all the authority of a monarch, and a very autocratic one at that."

"Of course it can be argued," said Gisela. "That's why the prophecy was still hanging about you when you arrived in Arville." She looked at Ember. "Speaking of the island, we were interrupted in our conversation yesterday. Where did things stand when you left there?"

"Everything was still very much in flux," Ember admitted. "I wish I could say it was a clean break, and everyone was happy to have the truth come out. But there are plenty who don't want to let go of the old ways, and would prefer to live in isolation." She shrugged. "That's not really an option now, though, with the barrier gone. And I confess, I'm glad of it."

Haiden nodded. "The island community is well set up to

prosper. With the regal onyx mine, they'll be able to trade very profitably with the mainland. And we intend to do all we can to ensure they're not exploited, and the mine isn't seized by enterprising arrivals from the mainland."

Gisela nodded. "Yes, as you asked, Otto's already written to Matthias to seek his support in that." She named the crown prince of Vadolis, the kingdom in which Arville was found. "I must say," she added, looking sideways at Haiden, "I was pleasantly surprised that you asked for Otto's help, and in turn Prince Matthias's."

"Yes, well, asking for help is something I'm trying to get better at," Haiden said.

"I make him practice in the looking glass three times a day," Ember chimed in cheekily.

Haiden swatted at her, but maintained his comfortable hold on her arm.

"They're working on a new structure of leadership on the island, and it will be much better than what was there before. Although they decided to send the Protector's brother to the capital of Vadolis to face justice, they're mostly hoping to remain autonomous."

"Yes, and ironically, it's looking like Gil will be one of the new leaders," Ember added. She grinned at Gisela. "I could have been the wife of a ruler too, in a way."

"And instead," said Haiden, "you wasted your time breaking my curse. And in spite of rumor, for all your efforts you got no magical prize whatsoever."

"Well," said Ember comfortably, "that's a matter of perspective, really."

"My word." A cheerful new voice made them all turn, to see Gisela's husband, Prince Otto, right behind them. "This is a whole new angle on you, Haiden. I never imagined you could be so soppy and sentimental." His pleasant face split into a grin. "It's beautiful. Frankly, I've never felt closer to you."

Haiden couldn't help but laugh. Privately he used to think Otto too sentimental back when they'd first met. Now he understood a little more.

"Well, it sounds like the island will be in good hands once the dust settles," Gisela said, responding to the hearty demands of her infant son and handing him off to his father. She watched fondly for a moment as Otto made theatrical faces, much to the baby's delight, then she turned back to Haiden and Ember.

"It also sounds like you're not planning to return there permanently."

"We're not," Haiden confirmed. "We don't know exactly what's next for us. We'll stay here for a bit, if we're welcome."

"Always," Gisela and Otto said together.

Haiden smiled. "After that, well, Ember's eager to see more of Providore, which suits me perfectly. And then...who knows?"

He exchanged a look with his wife. There was a little more to their plans. He hadn't fully given up on his idea of reaching the Reviled Lands one day, and Ember wasn't against the idea herself.

Haiden no longer felt the need to run away from his past, or the need for answers about the land of his ancestors to find peace with his present. But he was still curious, and with the barrier gone, it might be possible to sail to the smaller continent. The barrier may have been put in place to protect the island from discovery. But it had also had the effect of keeping anyone from sailing past to the Reviled Lands.

Attempting any such voyage wasn't an imminent plan,

though, and Haiden and Ember had decided not to mention it to Otto and Gisela. It might be fraught, given the other couple were royals, and there was still a prohibition in place on contact between Providore and the Reviled Lands. A prohibition that had been inadvertently reinforced by the existence of the magical barrier, which had seemed to give force to the ban.

All that was far in the future, anyway. For now, there was plenty to be discovered on the continent they already knew. It hadn't taken much of the journey from Arville to Terenford for Haiden to learn that nothing brought him such joy as seeing Ember's excitement every time she discovered a new place or an unfamiliar landscape.

He intended to show her as much of it as he could, from the enormous wall that separated the frozen north from the even more frozen land of the giants, to the heat of the southern shores, off which the great mermaid empire had been discovered not so many years before.

With Ember, every step would be an adventure. It had already begun, and he could hope for nothing better than for it to never end.

*Island of Secrets and Sacrifice is book 4 in the* Sacrificed Hearts *multi-author series, a collection of stand-alone fantasy romances inspired by monsters of legend, each tale packed with strong heroines, swoony heroes, and sacrificial themes. Read the next adventure in* Assassin of Fire and Sacrifice *by Mary Mecham.*

# DON'T MISS THE NEXT BOOK!

## ASSASSIN OF FIRE AND SACRIFICE

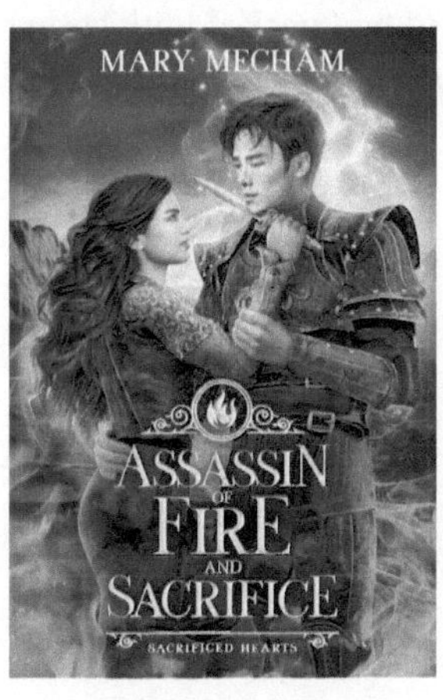

**To assassinate her target, she must marry her enemy.**

Azora has dedicated her life to exacting revenge on the phoenix shifters who murdered her parents. When Prince Tarquin of Pyren demands a bride as part of a peace treaty, the elite strike squad of assassins Azora belongs to agree—she's the perfect candidate to eliminate the monstrous shifter.

The traces of Pyrenese blood flowing in her veins grant her immunity to fire and will allow her to slay Tarquin, for a phoenix can only be destroyed by one descended from Pyren. The safety of all Termarth is dependant on Azora to maintain her cover; her true identity must never be discovered.

With the tantalizing offer of peace on the altar, Azora weds Tarquin, knowing that as soon as the peace treaty is broken, either bride or groom will be the first casualty. But just as Azora begins to uncover the man behind the monster, skirmishes erupt throughout the land. When the time arrives to finally eliminate the threat to Termarth, Azora's loyalties are torn.

She intended to gamble her life away, not her heart.

*Assassin of Fire and Sacrifice is book 5 in the* Sacrificed Hearts *multi-author series, a collection of stand-alone fantasy romances inspired by monsters of legend and packed with strong heroines, swoony heroes, and sacrificial themes.*

Find the book on Amazon today!

## NOTE FROM THE AUTHOR

Thank you for reading *Island of Secrets and Sacrifice*. I hope you enjoyed visiting the world of Providore. I would be so grateful if you would consider leaving a review on Amazon —it would really make a difference!

If you've yet to read the previous adventures set on the continent of Providore, check out *The Singer Tales* today! This completed series includes six connected but stand-alone fairy tale retellings featuring strong heroines navigating everything from miniature elves to brutish giants as they chase their own happily ever afters.

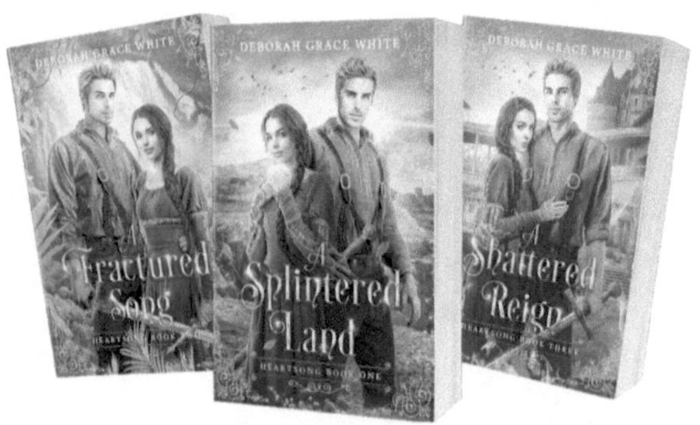

*When a singer with too many questions meets a farmer hiding dangerous answers, past and present collide and heart is pitted against duty.*

If you want more adventure, magic, and clean and swoony romance in this world where magic is harnessed by singers, check out *Heartsong*. This YA fantasy trilogy is set in the Sovereign Realms, which the people of Providore call The Reviled Lands (but requires no prior reading).

Join up to my mailing list at deborahgracewhite.com to be kept up to date on new releases, specials, and giveaways, such as bonus chapters. You'll receive some great freebies, too, including *An Expectation of Magic*, a novella which is a prequel to my completed YA fantasy series *The Vazula Chronicles*.

Plus, you'll receive *Dragon's Sight*, an 8,000 word prequel to my completed YA fantasy trilogy *The Kyona Chronicles*.

Again, thanks for entering the world of Providore! I hope to see you back again.

# ALSO BY DEBORAH GRACE WHITE

The Kyona Chronicles: YA Fantasy

The Kyona Legacy: YA Fantasy

*Also by Deborah Grace White*

## The Vazula Chronicles: YA Fantasy

## The Kingdom Tales: Fairy Tale Retellings

## The Singer Tales: Fairy Tale Retellings

## The Unlucky Prince: Fairy Tale Retelling
## (Once Upon a Prince Multi-Author Series)

# ACKNOWLEDGMENTS

Thank you so much to everyone who helped make *Island of Secrets and Sacrifice* a reality!

Firstly, to Tara Grayce and Everly Haywood for organizing this multi-author series and inviting me to join. And to Callie Thomas, Mary Mecham, and CFE Black for being so awesome to work with! It's been loads of fun, and I'm really proud of the series we've produced.

I also want to thank my usual team. Ray, my husband and first support, you're the best. My betas: Mel W, Tricia, Adrian, Catherine, and Dad, thanks for your invaluable feedback and for improving the story! Shae for the usual fantastic proofread. Any remaining errors are mine.

Thanks to Moorbooks for the gorgeous cover, which perfectly captured both Haiden and Ember, and to Becca for the map.

To you, the reader, thank you for giving me the privilege of being an author.

And most importantly, to God, who never turns his back on us when we turn to him for help.

# ABOUT THE AUTHOR

I've been a reader since I can remember, growing up on a wide range of books, from classic literature to light-hearted romps. The love of reading has traveled with me unchanged across multiple continents, and carried me from my own childhood all the way to having children of my own.

But if reading is like looking through a window into a magical and beautiful world, beginning to write my own stories was like discovering that I could open that window and climb right out into fantasyland.

I cannot believe how privileged I am to actually be living that childhood dream and publishing my own novels. I do so from my hometown of Adelaide, Australia, where I live with my husband and our four little ones.

I've never outgrown my love of young adult stories, so the genre of young adult fantasy was always going to be my niche. Feel free to email me at deborah@deborahgrace white.com and introduce yourself! Or subscribe to my mailing list at deborahgracewhite.com for free giveaways, sales, and updates.

www.ingramcontent.com/pod-product-compliance
Lightning Source LLC
Chambersburg PA
CBHW051306210726
48287CB00002B/706